THE DANGERS OF

EVERYDAY LIFE

New Atlantic Media
Chapel Hill, NC
2022

THE DANGERS OF EVERYDAY LIFE

LINKED STORIES

PETER FILENE

Also By PETER FILENE

Personal Histories

Striving Fathers, Troubled Sons: From John Adams to James Baldwin

The Joy of Teaching: A Practical Guide for New College Instructors

Him/Her/Self: Gender Identities in Modern America

In the Arms of Others: A Cultural History of the Right to Die

Home and Away (a novel)

Men in the Middle: Work and Family in the Lives of Middle-Aged Men

Americans and the Soviet Experiment, 1917-1933

ISBN 978-1-737-5336-1-0

Book Design by Tim Hubbard
New Atlantic Media
Chapel Hill, NC
NewAtlanticMedia2002@gmail.com

Printed in the United States of America
10 9 8 7 6 5 4 3 2 1

"The Relics of Vince Delaney" appeared in different form
in Carolina Quarterly (Winter 1988)
"Venial Sins" appeared in Cimarron Review (January 1993)

For Stuart
 With love.

CONTENTS

ACKNOWLEDGMENTS

"Thank you" doesn't come close to saying what I owe my writing group: Laurel Goldman, Peggy Payne, Angela Davis-Gardner, Joe Burgo and Christina Askounis as well as, back when, Pete Hendricks, Linda Orr and Dorrie Casey.. Every Thursday afternoon since time out of mind, I've looked forward to your invaluable critiques and unfailing friendship.

And thank you, John Kasson, for your thoughtful suggestions.

Finally, thank you, Tim Hubbard, for designing this book with devotion to details, openness to suggestions, and flair.

INTRODUCTION

I wrote this set of linked stories in the 1980s, half my lifetime ago. Two were published in small literary magazines, while the others were rejected again and again until I put them to rest in my file cabinet and moved on to more hopeful projects.

Why publish them now? Not for fortune or fame, but for the sake of the characters in these stories. I created them and, through all these years, have harbored a parental affection and pride toward them. They deserve to be brought into the light of the world—if not now, when.

In many ways they are historical artifacts. They rely on typewriters and phone books and listen to Michael Jackson on transistor radios. They would be mystified by allusions to 9/11 or transgender. I could, with a lot of effort, try to bring them up to date. But no, they belong to their era and also, I should say, to my middle age. In these stories I was reckoning with the aftermath of much personal turbulence—divorce, frustrations with career, artistic fantasies.

I can't imagine how I managed to write fiction amid all my day-to-day responsibilities. I was, after all, a professor of U.S. history, teaching a hundred-plus students three times a week about real people (and also the father of two teenagers). Yet there I sat for hours in my tiny "study" on the eighth floor of the library writing about people who seemed to me equally real, maybe more real. Al and Anna Cox, Sam Jacobson and the other inhabitants of this collection bore traces of my friends and experiences. They also carried some of my confusions and hopes and regrets. But ultimately they became altogether themselves.

Consider Vince Delaney, for example, with a wife and five cats and the biography of Rousseau he'll never finish writing, as he calculates his venial sins. Anna Cox once yearned to follow Joni Mitchell's footsteps to the Mermaid Tavern on the coast of Crete, but remains landlocked in North Carolina as an aerobics instructor. Charles Weber, the editor of *The Almanac of Has-Beens*, feels abandoned as his daughter departs for college.

In the end, all these characters will find a path out of their dilemma to claim a new direction, a renewed understanding of self. Here they are at last, inviting you to share their hardwon accomplishments.

Mr. and Mrs. Thoreau

The first summer, it took them all afternoon to pack the car. Sitting on deck chairs in the yard, they held up one book after another for consent or veto until, by dinner time, they had filled the trunk with fiction. They drove north to his cabin in Rhinebeck with stacks of Virginia Woolf, Saul Bellow and Margaret Atwood wedged around the spare tire. "Let's not stop until we get there," she said, and for eleven hours they were a couple of joyriders speeding along the Interstates. The next day, lying naked in the ripe grass beside the well house, he asked, "Are you happy?"

"Guess," she said as her nipples stiffened, and they made leisurely love.

The second summer was supposed to be their Continental Classics summer, but along with Tolstoy and Flaubert she wanted bestsellers by women. So they followed their new rule, filling the trunk with books they agreed on and the back seat with everything else. After lunch they swung in separate hammocks, reading aloud until darkness pushed them indoors. After dinner they played gin rummy for dimes, and by August she owed him a fortune. One night she whooped with her orgasm and an owl whooped back.

The third summer they divided the trunk down the middle, one side for his biographies and gardening books, the other for her cookbooks and dream books. In the mornings she baked corn muffins and fritters, carrot cakes, banana puddings frothing with meringue. "You're getting plump," he said, thumbing crescent moons on her thigh. "Don't," she said, pushing his hand away.

The last summer they went to Rhinebeck, he had no idea it would be the last. For weeks he didn't guess, although he heard Michael Jackson spilling out of her boombox in the house and down to the stream where he was fishing. Didn't guess even while he watched her knitting the white sweater night after night. Even when Mitchell drove up in that French sports car, panicking the squirrels with three blithe toots of the horn, he didn't understand what was happening. It was all done before he assembled his frenzy into words.

At the end of the last summer, here he is, sitting at the kitchen table, writing a story that makes no sense. It only adds to the baffled pain. *If the teeth ache, they can be pulled. If the heart aches, what then?*—Thoreau.

At the top of a new page he writes:

Clues to Why She Left

An hour later, when nothing has happened, he crosses out "She" and puts in "The Bitch," and then down the left edge:

First,

Second,

Third,

Fourth.

First, the day she moved in, she kicked everything off his coffee table. On their wedding day she paused in the middle of making a phone call. Had they spoken their fears, what would have happened instead?

Second, she screamed: "You're not my teacher any more." If he had heard what she meant, might he have been the first to leave?

Third was the summer it rained so much and they wore clothes. A cold continuous rain. Through half of August he coughed in the spare room.

Fourth, Mitchell arrived. The smiling trespasser. After the two of them drove away, he sat up all night in an empty house saying her name.

Anna drove away, leaving behind everything she owned.

Anna made and unmade his life like a bed.

Anna whom he bitterly loved.

The kitchen table is slippery under his forearms. Since sunset, the thermometer's red hand hasn't budged from ninety-two. Heat lightning wrinkles the dead-black sky.

"Fool's rain," they call it in these parts.

In the end he still doesn't understand why it's come out this way and not some other way. He closes his eyes and listens to the empty thunder in the hills.

Maybe the problem is he's telling the end of the story instead of the story. So he begins again at the top of a new page, pretending this time he doesn't know where it comes out.

· · ·

The first summer, in 1981, when they went up to Rhinebeck on their honeymoon, everything was falling exactly into place.

In February, Carl had signed the agreement deeding him the cabin in exchange for Dad's life insurance and '79 Pontiac. The portables, his brother called them. "Give me a choice between three-point-five godforsaken acres under a shack or portables," Carl said in his brisk salesman's voice, "and I'll take the portables every time."

"Cabin," he replied before he could stop himself. "Not a shack—a cabin."

"Whatever. If Dad had just burned it down along with the barn, it wouldn't be anything at all."

"That was lightning, Carl. The sheriff said—"

"Yeah, yeah, I know that story. Hey, kid, got to hang up."

In March, Anna beckoned him to the empty seat beside her at the Varsity Theater where he had fled from grading midterm exams to watch *The Big Chill*.

Afterwards they went to a bar and talked about themselves. She was working in the art supply shop at the mall until something better came along; she loved the way he used to read poems too loud in class; and yes, her blond hair was really blond. He owned a cabin like Thoreau's and was hoping to write a book some day, a great book, about Hawthorne and Emerson. Her hand rested like a familiar animal inside his. He felt undefended—frightened of falling in love with a young woman he'd known for all of one semester in "Classic American Lit." She'd gazed up at him from the front row, her large blue eyes absorbing his words, until shortly before the end of the hour she would raise her hand and make a statement that invariably cut to the heart of things.

He squeezed her hand. "It's been a wonderful evening," he said.

"Come home with me," she said.

"The most fearless woman I've ever known," he declared in the dark after they made love.

"In that case, you've known mighty few women," she said, running a finger along his spine. "Which I don't believe for a second."

At age thirty-two he'd been to bed with three women and in love with none. It was as if he'd been waiting for her. "I want to know you," he said. "Only you."

A week later she moved into his house. It took less than an hour to transfer her belongings. "I like the kind of woman who can pack twenty-two years of life into six cardboard boxes and a backpack," he said, planting the last box on the living-room rug.

She stepped out of her clogs, flexed her calf muscles, and raised her arms straight up. "When I got my first period, my mother sat me down and said: 'Save your treasure for a husband who'll give you love and a big house'—another of her slams at Dad. I told her, 'I'm not going to own but five boxes in my life.' And she slapped me."

As she folded at the waist, her blond hair cascaded upon the rug and her upside-down voice came out thickly. "I'll have to throw away one box."

He patted her butt. "Keep it, sweetie, and if your mother visits, we'll say it's mine."

She straightened up, pink-cheeked. "Don't."

"Don't what?"

"Don't 'sweetie' me."

He laughed. "I didn't mean to offend the lady."

"I'm serious."

"How about 'honey'?"

Her eyes narrowed, and with one bare foot she swept the coffee table clean of books, unanswered letters, and the blue jug filled with daffodils. "This is a mistake. I'm getting out of here."

"No," he said. "Stay," he said more loudly, excited by the violence. "I dare you to stay."

In April he typed the dedication page of *The Great Failures of Thoreau* ("For my father, who would have understood") and then stared at the blank title page. "Should I be Albert W. or Albert Wentworth or just plain Albert Cox?" he called out to Anna in the living room.

"What would Thoreau prefer?" she called back.

In May they were married in the basement of the courthouse. The magistrate's office was so small that the five of them—the magistrate, Anna and Al, Mary Ellen and Austin—had to stand shoulder to shoulder around the desk. He memorized the angle of the hair across her forehead, that nick in the left front tooth, the smudge of ink on the knuckle above the new gold ring, the pulse trembling like crazy in the well of her throat. Anna Cameron. Anna Cameron Cox. He wanted her. He felt greedy to be taking in every detail of her. But she and this potbellied agent of the state of North Carolina had granted him the right to this greed, hadn't they? He wanted her with a hunger hollowing his chest. Before it was too late, he ought to clear up this question of greed. But all he said was "I do."

A storm had come and gone while they had been marrying inside, so the four of them held hands jumping over puddles to the car. At the edge of the courthouse lot, with the windows curtained by steam, Mary Ellen pulled out a joint. At first he coughed, because he hadn't smoked dope in so long, and then he smoothly got stoned along with the others. He hardly knew Mary Ellen, who had been Anna's college roommate. Anna hardly knew Austin, who was his best friend, or maybe his only friend, in the English Department. But as they drove across town, loudly applauding every green traffic light, he felt among lifelong buddies.

"Who carries whom over the threshold?" he asked her as he turned the front-door key.

"Whoomm," she hummed with her eyes closed as she rode upon his arms into their house. They bumped against walls, knocking pictures awry, and collapsed giggling on the couch.

She picked up the phone. "I should call my folks and get it over with. Baptists think eloping is as bad as fucking, you know."

"There's no telephone up in Rhinebeck. No TV, no neighbors. Nothing but you and me."

The receiver hovered in midair, inches from her open mouth, trembling. Then she shook her head and began to dial, as if she'd decided not to ask a difficult question. And he decided not to ask her about it for fear of disturbing their newly married house.

She told them she'd gotten married this morning, yes, that professor, no, he was only thirty-two, no, don't be silly, Mother, of course the university wouldn't fire him, oh for chrissake, why can't you just once. . . ?

For fifteen minutes he sat in his study where he could faintly hear her voice but couldn't snatch the phone from her hands and throw it against the wall. Then she was curled on his lap, red-eyed, whispering, "Hold me tight, Al. What have we done? Tell me I'll be all right."

So he told her until she took a deep breath and phoned her parents a second time. "You've had your turn and now it's mine. I'm married and I hope you'll invite us to dinner so you can meet my husband and maybe, God knows, even like him. And if you don't, then you don't, but no more of your carping." He lost hold of the shoe he was taking off when he heard her say "my husband."

Later he wrote identical notes to his mother and her boyfriend in Miami and to Carl and his latest wife in Orlando, saying they were in for a big surprise, the lifelong bachelor of the family was no more, having fallen in love with Anna, who was brilliant, exciting, and as the enclosed photo proved, beautiful. Come north and see for yourselves!!

He regretted the exclamation marks, because they revealed the lie of that sentence and cast doubt on his description of her. But he didn't care what his mother and brother thought. "You're a hopeless idealist just like your father," Mom used to say, "and look what it got him: a plaque from the company." Dad was dead now, and his younger son was married, and neither needed to defend themselves.

Their first wedded night, he couldn't fall asleep. He tried counting her singsong breaths but they only awakened him more. In his bachelor life he would have listened to jazz on the radio. As a husband, he tiptoed to the kitchen and saddle-soaped a pair of boots and wrote: *"The stones are happy, Concord River is happy, and I am happy too"—so said Thoreau.*

Yawning, he taped the little paper to the coffee pot. In the morning it hung on the refrigerator. *"Same here," says Mrs. T.,* it said in pencil at the bottom.

A month later they sat all afternoon on deck chairs in the front yard, holding up fiction and preparing for their honeymoon. Then at last they were lying naked in Rhinebeck under the warm sun.

"How many other sexy former students have laid in this spot?" she asked.

"Don't worry. After Dad died and my mother followed Carl down to Florida, I didn't want anybody here, sexy or not."

"Don't they ever want to come up, your mom and brother?"

"No, and if they did, I wouldn't let them. They belong in Florida."

"So it's just for us. A kingdom for two."

He propped himself on an elbow. "Are you happy?"

"Guess," she said. But it was a summer when he didn't have to guess.

. . .

The second summer they filled the trunk with European authors and argued over bestsellers by women. "There's no room for pop lit," he said.

"If we take out your Tolstoy and Hugo, we'd have room."

"Anne Tyler's charming, but charm doesn't add up to literature."

"Cool it, mister. You don't set my reading assignments any more."

He kicked a dent in the fender and they didn't say a word to each other until the next morning, when they invented a new rule. The trunk was reserved for the things they could agree on, and on the back seat they stuffed as much of everything else as would fit.

Early that summer he put up the two hammocks between the big oaks by the creek. In the elbow of one branch he fashioned spare boards into a shelf for books, playing cards, and bug spray. Five feet above the ground he screwed in hooks for hanging her baseball cap and his John Deere cap. In a right angle around the trunk he made the narrow table, really more a counter than a table, that he constructed from some two-by-sixes that had survived the barn fire. Underneath he set milk crates to hold two dishes, two cups, and the two hollow-stemmed glasses they'd bought from his mother's wedding check. He did all of it one afternoon while she was in town buying groceries. Did it in a series of sure strokes, hammering every nail true, fulfilling the images that had been waiting in his mind when he awoke at sunrise.

She jumped out of the car, stood between the hammocks, and began to weep. "Every Christmas I used to wish for a tree house," she said, "but there were no trees big enough in our yard. No place to hide." She laid her cheek on his sawdust-flecked chest. "I love you."

They swung in their hammocks through windless

afternoons. They took turns reading *War and Peace* until the hum of nineteenth-century sentences and cicadas put one of them to sleep. "You lose, you lose," the other one shouted triumphantly, and the loser had to wade into the bone-cold stream to fetch the bottle of white wine.

"You cheat by reading too softly," he said after having fallen asleep the fifth afternoon in a row. His instep felt bruised by the icy water.

"It takes two to lose—one to speak and another to sleep. Catch," she said, tossing him a pear.

His hands jumped apart and the pear split open on the ground. "That's Thoreau, you quoted."

"No, it's me Anna."

But it was Thoreau, *A Week on the Concord and Merrimack Rivers*, the quotation he wrote on the blackboard the first day of every semester. *It takes two to speak the truth— one to speak and another to hear.* "So I actually taught you something out there on the front row," he said.

Bending down to pick up the shards of pear, awed to have heard his words—Thoreau's words—spoken by her voice, he didn't see her coming. She knocked him to the ground and straddled him. "That A was mine, not yours."

He touched her lips. "Of course."

Nevertheless, it had been Thoreau. "Listen hard," he told his students, brandishing a stanza of Frost or a paragraph of Melville or one of Faulkner's page-long sentences. "It takes two to speak the truth. Listen passionately and enter the words of the writer." Each semester he read more and said less. He left longer and longer silences between the readings, lagoons of silences. The best students dove for understanding, the worst drowned asleep in their chairs, and most of them drifted, rolling ballpoint pens between their palms, scratching their ankles, waiting for Professor Cox to tell them what to write down in their spiral notebooks.

. . .

The third summer they played double solitaire at night on the back porch, using the old tool shed door for a table. The cards snagged on the splintering wood, so they spread her plaid skirt as a tablecloth. "Look at that," he said. "In Rhinebeck we dress the furniture and undress ourselves." But she didn't smile. "Let's burn our clothes," he persisted, "and be naked all summer."

She held a fan of cards over the crotch of her leotard. "Going naked to town will be kind of tricky."

"Okay, an hour of clothes for grocery-shopping."

"What about movies?"

"We don't need movies."

"I like movies."

"Listen to me," he said more fiercely than he'd expected. He pointed over the well house and down the road. "Out there they want to straitjacket us in clothes and jobs and rules."

She laughed. "You sound like some leftover hippie."

"I'm serious."

"In that case, how about turning this place into a nudist camp? Al's Thoroughly Nudist Camp."

"Stop it."

She scribbled letters across the air. "Thoreau-ly nude."

He stood up and tossed the cards on the table. "You're not funny."

"And you're no fun."

In the morning they woke safely in each other's arms. But they didn't talk about the night before.

A Guide to Dreams. Personal Growth Through Your Dreams. The Art of Dreaming. She read glossy paperbacks in her hammock while he hacked at the weeds that crept toward the Brussels sprouts, which, for all he knew, might well have been the first Brussels sprouts anyone had ever dared plant in central New York State.

Each morning she lay with hands folded upon her stomach as she recounted her dreams. Long, zealous narratives featuring people from her past, surreal locales, and portentous symbols. He lay beside her, feeling excluded, thinking about Brussels sprouts. "I'm tired of hearing your dreams," he said at last.

"Tell some of your own, then."

"I can't remember them." All his life he had left his dreams behind him in the night, but until now he'd never missed them.

"Poor Al. Am I supposed to make dreams for you?"

As he brushed his teeth, he felt lonesome. He called his

name into the mirror very softly, like a faraway voice calling him for dinner. *Come ho-omm.* He and Carl would race along the creek past the well house, arms churning, until the first one to touch Dad's belt buckle won the extra dessert.

All morning he fished inside the lonesomeness and caught nothing. *Am I supposed to make dreams for you? Why not? Why not?* He leaned back against the boulder—the throne, he and Carl used to call it—and watched the hawk circling a thousand feet up. It rode the airwaves in silence, scanning for the twitch of some tiny rodent, shopping in circles for lunch.

Woe to him who wants a companion, Thoreau said, *for he is unfit to be the companion even of himself.*

Well, Thoreau could go fuck himself. This morning he wanted these three-point-five acres peopled by Anna and several sons and daughters tossing a Frisbee, fishing, picnicking, plus dogs and horses and maybe goats—a happy congregation.

The next morning he told it to her as his dream.

"That's lovely, but can you imagine someone actually growing inside me?" she said, plopping a pillow on her stomach. "I can't."

He could imagine it, vividly, but he didn't say so.

She baked corn muffins and carrot cakes (rehearsing for her job at Sweet Seasons) and he made salads of tomatoes and beans (waiting impatiently for the Brussels sprouts to ripen). She did push-ups and sit-ups while he read biographies of

Emerson. On Saturday nights they drove to town and saw the seven o'clock movie.

When he caught pneumonia and lay under a blanket in the spare room for half of August, coughing, he was too busy to be lonesome. He devoted full attention to coughing and the damage it might cause. As a cough climbed out of his lungs and scraped along his throat, he imagined the bruised tissue, the mangled membrane, wounds that would heal badly, if at all. Destruction was taking place. A fevered engine inside his chest was manufacturing shrapnel to slice and shred him. He was almost grateful that the coughs kept him awake, because then he had a better chance of defending himself. Holding his breath. Swallowing. Smothering that fiend in the darkness down there.

She said he'd been delirious for six hours, babbling words she couldn't make out. All night, she said, she'd laid cool cloths on his forehead and sung every song she could think of—lullabies, Beatles, hymns—until at dawn the fever broke and he recognized her again.

He held tight to her hand. "Thank you." All night he'd had her all to himself, full-time ardent attention, but he'd missed it. Maybe he should get pneumonia again, this time without delirium.

He lay like an old man in the spare room, drifting into and out of naps, day by day growing a little younger. "Sing to me," he said.

"I'll bring in the boombox, if you want."

He read or watched the clouds between naps. When he was strong enough, he walked in his bathrobe out to the garden and stood among the ragged, green-black leaves that had been Brussels sprouts. They made green ash between his fingers.

"You look like yourself again," she said one morning as she poured the coffee.

He realized, then, that she couldn't see the damage. Neither could the doctor. "Fit as a fiddle," the doctor said after tapping and listening. Nonetheless, when they returned to Chapel Hill from their third summer up in Rhinebeck, he was sure some harm had been done.

He tried describing it to Austin as they sat in his office for their coffee break. "First I don't dream and now I don't talk."

"Bullshit," Austin said. "Just listen to yourself talking about not talking. You're as verbose as the rest of us pedants." He poked him in the shoulder with a spoon. "You want my diagnosis? Post-tenure depression. For five years—ten or fifteen years if you count grad school—a guy works his ass to a nub to get tenure. And now that you've got it, you feel betrayed. It's like God sent you a telegram saying you're saved, but life goes on exactly as it did: midterm exams, electric bills, and your friend Austin telling you you're full of shit." With a glance at his watch, he stood up and put a hand on Al's shoulder. "Spend more time with Anna and less with Thoreau and I wager you'll feel fine in thirty days, my friend."

"Listen, friend." He shrugged off the hand. "Don't come

drinking my coffee until you're ready to take me seriously."

Austin gave him a long stare. Then he left, slamming the door.

Every afternoon at the end of her shift at Sweet Seasons, Anna slithered into a leotard and went to work out at The Body Shop. Three evenings a week she stayed there to teach aerobics classes. He grew used to the wrinkled leotard drying at night on the shower curtain rod like a pink or purple skin she had shed. There was big money in aerobics, she told him. She was thinking of joining up with a friend of Mary Ellen's who was building a spa of his own. She talked a new jargon: pecs and quads and reps. But even if it turned out to be another of her quick careers, it certainly did, as she said, keep her boobs firm. "You should try it, Al."

"Not my style." He had accompanied her once to The Body Shop and that was enough. All those people writhing in the grip of weird machines, gazing into the mirror while the electric music cheered them on. Everyone eyed everyone's body like avid shoppers.

"Go ahead and sneer," she said, "but cardio-vascular activity will add five years to your life."

"Some life. Those Body Shoppers don't care about inner life, just quads and pecs."

She pinched the jelly roll of flesh above his belt. "I'll be home by ten. I hope the writing goes well."

Write for yourself and strangers: Gertrude Stein. He had taped the quote over his desk after his book came out and the reviewers set to work on it with their buzz saws. "Cox approaches Thoreau in such eccentric ways that he never arrives within hailing distance." "Although Professor Cox raises brilliant questions, his answers are something else entirely." "The title of *Great Failures* says it all."

Write for yourself and strangers. *But when in doubt,* he scribbled below, *forget the strangers.* On Tuesday, Wednesday and Thursday nights, while Anna was teaching aerobics, he unplugged the phone, pushed back the empty dinner plate, and sat at the kitchen table writing for himself, *Concord's Feast of Fools.* Three years ago he had woken up with the title in his mind. He held on to it as he worked his way through monographs by anthropologists, theologists, and cultural historians, rereading Melville, Emerson and Hawthorne, typing stacks of index cards, watching the evidence assemble into a feast of fools, the mocking festival that greeted each new year of the Middle Ages. With the research completed, he began to write. Tightly strung sentences. Paragraphs soaring with theory and tethered by quotes. A magnum opus, if he could pull it off.

When he could no longer focus his eyes, he put the empty dinner plate on top of the pages. The jazz raveling from the radio loosened his mind as he drank a beer and waited for Anna to come home. All night his mind slept in utter silence. At breakfast he read with amazement what he had written. He wouldn't let anyone read it until he felt a little more certain how crazed it would seem.

The momentum of writing carried him almost absentmindedly through classes and faculty meetings and conversations with people in the halls. He stopped reading newspapers. He drove to and from campus with a notebook in his lap, scribbling ideas at red lights.

Austin knocked on his office door one morning. "Howdy, Professor," he said, turning his empty cup upside down. "Let's share a hit of caffeine."

"I just finished mine." He held his finger on the page he'd been reading.

"You got a few minutes to talk?"

"I'm getting ready for my Modern Novel seminar."

"Listen, friend, what I have to say is more important than Faulkner."

But the writing wouldn't let go of him. Held him like a grudge. He didn't want Austin's gossip and jokes and rolling laugh. "No thanks. Another time."

"You stubborn son of a bitch. If I weren't such a noble guy, I'd piss on your desk. Don't talk with me, then, but I suggest you talk with your wife."

"What about?"

"Ask her," he said over his shoulder as he walked away.

By April he was writing on Tuesday, Wednesday, Thursday and Sunday nights. By May he had added Friday night. He had never written so purely. A hundred and fifty pages by June. He graded final exams, slept for thirteen hours, and mailed *Concord's Feast of Fools* to Harvard University Press. "It's time to fish and make love," he said to Anna.

· · ·

The last summer they put the boombox in the back seat alongside the ice chest and fishing rods. He heard the aerobic beat all the way down at the stream. As he stood fishing, he sometimes imagined the cicadas were pulsing in time with Michael Jackson. He hated the noise. It fell from the porch like DDT from a crop-duster plane, poisoning everything. She consented to turn it off after lunch, but in the midst of weeding the garden he heard himself whispering, "beat it, just beat it."

Tomatoes, beans and cucumbers, but no Brussels sprouts. He didn't have sufficient faith this summer.

She'd cut her hair short, a jagged margin around her ears. It was as if she'd pulled the roots deeper into her skull. He wasn't used to seeing the back of her neck, where the tendons stood out like an extra pair of vocal cords. Her body was so supple and sure of itself now. "That's tone you're touching," she bragged, propping one foot against the bureau. He began to invent a joke about making love with a touch-tone telephone, but gave up halfway through.

After dinner, she knit and he read. She knit for hours until the furious click-clicking of the needles became another background music along with the bullfrogs. One evening she held up a blue-and-white striped sweater but didn't ask him to try it on. Then she began a scarf. A sweater and scarf in the middle of summer? Anyone else would have asked whom she was knitting them for, but he was afraid of what she might answer.

At the beginning of July she said, "Don't you ever feel lonely up here?"

"Not with you around."

"Let's go into town for the fireworks this year. Get drunk and sit on the high school football field going ooh and ahh along with everyone else."

"We can see the fireworks from here. Get drunk on our lawn, just the two of us."

She looked down as she kneaded a calf muscle. "Al, how would you feel if I invited a friend to come up and visit?"

She stopped kneading but didn't look up. The cords behind her neck throbbed. He couldn't read her face to know what she meant.

"Okay," he said at last, because he had to say it. "What the hell," he said, gathering up some heartiness. "Mother and Carl's ghosts have hung around here long enough. Time for a real guest." It was the right answer; she was nodding and smiling now. "Whom did you have in mind?" he asked, and then, terrified, he said, "Mary Ellen—good idea," before she could answer. But the terror kept rising in him and he rushed outside into the open air.

A friend! She had someone in mind—a person with face and clothing and voice—whereas he had only the blank word, "friend." And if there was one friend, there could be more—strangers whom she called friends. Certain bodies had stopped writhing in the Body Shop and exchanged names with her. Certain customers in Sweet Seasons had become familiar faces who had coffee with her. A crowd inhabited her mind. Without his noticing it, she had packed her mind full of friends to carry up to Rhinebeck.

He lay in the hammock, arms stiff at his side. They had made a mistake. At some point during the past four years they had misread a crucial signal. Damage had been done. But it wasn't too late. This afternoon he had heard her, clear as a warning shout. A friend! As soon as he figured out what had gone wrong, he would be her friend.

"What are you doing, Al?"

"Getting some air."

She swung in the other hammock, eyes shut against the sun. "We have to talk, Al."

The terror grabbed his throat. "Later."

"Soon," she said softly. "We have to talk very soon."

The softness, that pretense of kindness, hit him square in the face. "Goddamn you," he shouted. "You've fucked up everything, you and your fucking pecs and quads."

She stood over him, a rigid silhouette. "Don't ever talk to me like that again." Her calf muscles and buttocks worked serenely beneath her beautiful skin as she walked away.

Two days later he was still trying to placate her when Mitchell drove up in a red sports car. Craig Mitchell, hotshot of the history department, national award winner, fast talker, smiling and blond. Of all the possible strangers, how did she find this one?

"Hi there, Albert. Craig Mitchell here. You and I met at Dean Schafer's party, you may recall." He reached out to shake hands, and when he found no hand to shake, he reached into the pocket of his windbreaker and pulled out a pack of cigarettes. "Where's Anna?"

She stood on the top step, staring down at them. "Go drive down the road and back, Craig. I'll be ready soon."

Ready soon. They could talk, but she was saying how it would end—that it had already ended sometime ago. It was no use, but he would go through with the talking nonetheless. Because he had nothing else. Because if she explained it to him, at least he would understand why he was going through the most awful day of his life.

"I tried to warn you," she was saying. "I even asked Austin to tell you. . . ."

"Like that night after Easter," she was saying, picking up the saltshaker and putting it down, picking it up and putting it down. "Let's kick up some dust for a change, I said, but you. . . ."

"I met him last March in the whirlpool," she was saying, sparing him the sound of Craig Mitchell's name. "We just started talking, about Jack Nicholson movies, and then he asked me to have a cup of coffee. But he wasn't the reason. I was already. . . ."

"I'm not in love with him," she was saying as she stuffed jeans and a shirt and socks into her backpack. "I just need a vacation."

He thought of hugging her, but that seemed dangerous. He wanted to throw her on the bed, press her shoulders flat against the mattress, and force love back into her until she was sobbing his name and Craig Mitchell wasn't honking his horn in the driveway.

All at once she was gone. The house bulged with emptiness. He went from room to room. He sat in chairs and got up, sat and got up. He wished he chewed gum or smoked cigarettes. The wispy sound of his breathing got on his nerves, so he went down to the shed and hammered bent nails out of boards, making as much noise as possible. But when he came back, the house remained empty. He wasn't hungry. He wasn't sleepy. He wasn't anything.

Off and on he spoke her name and then, late at night, he lit the hurricane lamp and began to write. One false start. Another. And finally, pretending this time he didn't know where it came out, he settled down to write the story of his marriage.

.   .   .

It's done now. Twenty-seven pages. Four-twenty a.m. "As well done as a fifteen-minute egg," Dad used to say. Heat lightning slices feverishly across the sky.

He wads the pages into a yellow ball and hookshoots it into the trashcan. The next moves come easily. Into the can he stuffs her aerobics sweatshirt, the gray one inscribed "Body Shop," and the bright green leotard, lizard green in the yellow hurricane lamplight, and the tennis shoes, even though all that rubber won't catch. Then the yellow robe, which settles softly into the can like a drowsy pet. His own robe next, folding inside the folds of hers, blue and yellow, yellow and blue. A skein of white yarn, a skein of blue. The photo of her laughing on the porch, the photo of himself pointing at the freshly tilled garden. And finally the books: swaybacked Tolstoy; slim poetry volumes; dream books; cookbooks; Virginia Woolf's journal skewered with bookmarks. He hesitates over *The Great Failures*, shrugs, and drops it on top of Virginia Woolf.

One ten-gallon can of goods. It doesn't add up to much. They've been faithful to Thoreau's command: *Simplify, simplify*. He will stay faithful. Sweat slides down his face as he puts his arms around the can and wrestles it through the doorway, down the steps, into the moonless night. He almost loses his grip crossing the grass slick with dew, but he holds on, heaving and grunting, tasting salt. The hammocks hang across the darkness like pale smiles. Far away a loon laughs.

For a long time he stands, waiting for words, while his feet cool against the grass. Nothing comes. Finally he strikes a match. It flickers against a book and dies. He rips out pages, strikes another match, and this time they catch, followed by the yarn, smoldering blue, and then with an exuberant gush the nylon leotards blow hot life into it all. Cinders leap into the night. Owls flap away. He runs to the car and gathers fuel: road maps, oil rags, a roll of cherry lifesavers, her sun glasses. Spitting and popping, the flames grab a hammock.

Did Thoreau write something pithy about understanding through fire? Then he remembers his admonition to graduate students: *Never end your thesis with someone else's words. Say goodbye in your own voice.*

"Goodbye," he shouts as the hammock shrivels into a web of ash. "Goodbye," again and again, until he begins to believe himself.

ANNA'S TURN

"Humphrey is still swimming up the Sacramento River," the newscaster says.

Anna's only half-awake, half-listening to the radio, clutching the pillow as if it's a man. In two hours she's due in court to be divorced. After a year of being separated, you'd think this last snip of the cord to Al would be no big deal. "A mere formality," her lawyer said, but this morning it grabs her by the throat. They used to read Tolstoy aloud to each other in their hammocks. He tongued her breasts murmuring "lovely." She felt so wanted. So safe.

"It's been ten days now since the wayward whale made a left turn when he should have kept swimming straight south."

Maybe she should phone Craig to say she'd changed her mind, would he please accompany her after all. "If that's what you want," he'd say. What does she want? She pictures herself and Craig walking into the courthouse, shoulder to shoulder but not holding hands, because he thinks that's clichéd. He'd be doing his clumsy caretaker best, delivering a mini-lecture about divorce in early Modern Europe to "take your mind off yourself, honey."

She tosses the pillow to the floor. Well, at least she knows what she doesn't want. She needed Craig to escort her out of marriage, but she'll do divorce on her own.

"Oceanologists can't explain his peculiar behavior. But the longer he stays in fresh water, they say, the greater the danger of severe eye problems."

She imagines bulky, gray Humphrey peering curiously at the people gawking from the riverbank. Poor Humphrey. She turns off the radio and suddenly she's crying. A gush of tears, followed by snuffly sobs. She's supposed to be done with crying, isn't she? Twice a week for three months she used up Dr. Stern's Kleenex as she tried to understand why she'd jumped into Craig's red sport car and left her husband standing forlornly on the porch. Hour after hour she'd turned herself inside out until she finally made some kind of peace with her guilt. Yet here she is, leaking again.

Shape up, Anna. She marches into the bathroom, steps into the shower, lifts her face and lets the cool water stream down her eyelids. In California, with a wide-open ocean behind him, Humphrey is swimming upriver as if he has an appointment to keep. But at the end of the narrowing passage nothing awaits him. Worse than nothing.

She feels a dark wave of dread rolling toward her. Turn around, she calls from Chapel Hill on the other side of the continent.

. . .

By the time she finds a parking space downtown, the line outside the courthouse stretches halfway down the block. What crimes have brought all these people here this morning? She takes her place at the end of the line, avoiding the eyes of passersby, and opens *Joy Luck Club,* page twenty-six. The sun beats upon her head; perspiration trickles between her breasts. A mere formality, like getting a driver's license, but it feels like the last bit of punishment.

Finally the door opens and everybody shuffles inside.

She sits on a bench in the back and bends her head over page twenty-six.

"Hear ye, hear ye. Please rise for Judge Patricia Knowles." She stands as the black-robed woman strides toward her chair. "The court is now in session."

One and breathe, and two and breathe. Silently she recites the mantra she'll be chanting to her aerobics students at eleven o'clock. Three and breathe, and four and breathe.

"Anna Cameron Cox?"

Her cheeks hot, she walks up the aisle past the interested faces to the front of the room.

The clerk lays out two legal-sized pages on the desk.

Whereas the first party . . . per the aforesaid . . . whereas. . . . She pretends to read the mishmash, fast, wanting to get this over with, when suddenly some words leap off the creamy white surface: Albert Wentworth Cox and Anna Cameron Cox. She touches them with one finger, gently, but before she can figure out what she feels, the clerk is saying: "Sign here and here. Initial here."

She signs and signs and initials. He folds the pages. She slides them into her purse. Done. Her marriage is done with. Canceled as matter-of-factly as if she'd returned an electric mixer that didn't work.

As she steps outside, she's engulfed by sunlight and noise. Where did she park the car? She walks a few steps to the left, shakes her head, stops. Maybe it's back there. She turns and heads to the right.

Un-married. What does it mean to be un-married? But it's five minutes to ten and she doesn't have time to figure it out because she needs to find her car and get to a meeting at the Body Shop.

. . .

Cash flow. Before they can open a second Body Shop, Mr. Barnwell is saying, they need more cash flow. The three of them—she and Todd and their accountant—are jammed knee to knee in the back office, sipping nasty coffee out of Styrofoam cups. Todd clears his throat, studiously brushes nothing from the sleeve of his Ralph Lauren shirt, taps the pen against the ledger. "Okay, Mr. Barnwell, let's just stipulate a start-up loan at eight percent and. . . ."

For the last fifteen minutes she's said nothing beyond "Hello. Sorry I'm late." But that's okay, because she's trying to get her mind around being unmarried, and anyhow, god knows she doesn't understand cash flow. "I'll take care of the Body and you take care of the Shop." That was the deal she made with Todd when he hired her.

Maybe she should have studied accounting in college instead of novels. Then she could be contributing something intelligent to the discussion. What's more, then she'd never have met Albert Cox, professor of literature, and never have married him and left him. In college it didn't matter how often you changed majors. Sophomore year, she and Mary Ellen were geologists in October, anthropologists in January, before they split off into English and Elementary Ed. They laughed about it late at night, sitting cross-legged on their dorm beds with the joint passing back and forth and the candle making crazy movies on the wall.

Now, seven years later, she's a divorced aerobics instructor with a weekend "paramour," as Craig likes to put it, while Mary Ellen's the wife of an orthopedist with one kid and a second on the way. Out in the real world, changing majors isn't so easy.

"Okay, you put some numbers together and next week we'll get up with our lawyer to finalize this." Todd is standing, thumbs hooked in his vest. Mr. Barnwell is snapping his briefcase shut. Later on she'll ask Todd what was decided. Right now she needs to get out of this little office full of coffee breath.

The aerobics room is dark, silent; it might almost not be there. She stands at the edge of the nothingness, gropes along the wall for the buttons, and then—click, click, click—fluorescent light brings the room alive. The mirrored walls catch her and pass her on and multiply her as she walks over to the CD player. Electric guitars flood the silence, Whitney Houston begins to sing, and Anna's hips sway.

Soon the eleven o'clock class will arrive, and this room will fill with bodies encased in leotards. Mostly middle-aged women, even a few grandmothers: toothpaste tubes that have been unevenly squeezed. As the day goes on, the bodies will become less jiggly and lumpy, and the music will speed up. At 4:00 the high-school girls, rangy as young horses, prancing with Michael Jackson. After 5:00, it's Madonna for the college kids and the young professionals, strong, firm, sizing themselves up in mirrors, thinking ahead to drinks and dinner and sex. Every weekday they congregate and wait eagerly for her to make them proud. She welcomes them all, jiggly or firm.

She hums along with Whitney as she writes today's date on the sign-in page. Straightens a pile of towels. Checks the flow of the hot tub. Everything is ready for her salon ladies. She pulls off her leg warmers, smoothes a wrinkle in the purple leotard, and in the mirror catches herself smiling.

. . .

Craig has arrived for an overnight, wearing his familiar tweed sport jacket, with a bottle of Champagne in one hand and attaché case in the other. "Getting divorced deserves a celebration." He kisses her on the mouth. "And I've brought a surprise for you."

It's Thursday evening, not their usual weekend rendezvous time, but he phoned a few hours ago, saying "I bet you don't want to be alone tonight."

"That's sweet of you," she said, but now that he's here in her living room with Champagne and uncustomary solicitude and, presumably, sex on his mind, she's feeling a little crowded. Not literally. Craig's slender body doesn't take up much room and when he leaves on Sunday afternoons he removes all his belongings except for a toothbrush. "Don't worry, I have good boundaries," he announced the first time he slept over. Yes, just like his blond hair, which is parted evenly down the middle. After contending with moody Al, she likes Craig's distance. Tonight, though, her boundaries are shaky, and the Champagne isn't going to help.

"What's the surprise?" she says as they settle on the couch.

"Not yet. First a toast, if I can ever open this thing." He bends over the bottle, glasses sliding down his nose, tongue wedged between his lips. "Aha!" With a wet pop, the cork caroms off the wall, and he fills their glasses. "Santé to Anna Cameron."

"Thanks, although technically it's still Cox for another month."

The fizz climbs her nose, making her sneeze. The truth is she doesn't really care for Champagne.

"Gesundheit," he says. "So how did it go in court this morning?"

"Hard to say. Signing the actual document took all of sixty seconds. But seeing our names there, me and Al. . . . And being there with a judge. . . ." A fizzy sound bubbles out of her. "I felt guilty."

"But you're laughing. That's a good sign."

He pats her hand and she remembers that sadness makes him nervous, so she says: "What's my surprise?"

He snaps open the attaché case, rummages past the pajamas and pulls out a letter. "'Dear Professor Mitchell,'" he reads in a newscaster voice. "'Congratulations. The Fulbright Scholars Program is pleased to award you a year-long visiting professorship at the Université de Lyon, starting September 1.'" He waves the letter like a flag, smiling triumphantly.

"A year in France?"

"That's only half the story. Listen to this. 'Fulbright will pay for the travel and living expenses of a spouse.'" He sets the letter on the table. "What do you think, honey?"

She feels blank. "About what?"

"About being a spouse?"

"You mean married? But I thought . . . We never . . ." She can't make her words make sense.

"Surprise, surprise." He smiles and anger sweeps over her.

"For chrissake, Craig." She slams her glass on the table, spilling Champagne onto the letter. "What the hell are you doing? This morning I get divorced and you waltz in here tonight saying let's get married. That's a bad surprise. A bad stupid surprise."

"Actually, I got the letter two weeks ago, but I waited until you were a free woman."

"Not just get married, but go off to France for a year. What about my life? My classes?" She pictures her ladies stretching and bending, earnestly, proudly.

"If my students can do without me for a year, so can yours."

"But I don't have tenure. Todd may not hire me back."

"Hey, you said it wasn't a career."

She hates these kinds of discussions. He has all the answers, but they don't sound like the right answers. "I can't deal with this now."

"You've got a month to decide, darling." He takes off his glasses and strokes her arm. "Meanwhile, let's toast each other in bed."

"I don't know, Craig."

He leans back and squints at her. "What's the matter?"

"I think I want to be alone tonight."

Without glasses his face looks doughy. Vulnerable. "Well, if that's what you want." He puts on his glasses, stashes the letter behind the pajamas in the attaché case, snaps the buckles shut. "I'll see you tomorrow night, then."

"Okay. Maybe. I mean, let's talk tomorrow."

In bed she can't read the words on the page through the swirl of thoughts. France, wouldn't that be exciting, but married, Mrs. Mitchell, oh god, but if she says no, then a year alone and who knows.

. . .

Four days later, after traveling seventy miles upriver, Humphrey has stopped. But now he swims in circles, heedless of oceanologists banging metal pipes underwater. Scientists are increasingly worried about starvation from lack of seafood.

Mr. Barnwell has given the go-ahead for the second shop. Todd is on the phone for hours a day with banks and contractors, wheeling and dealing, chewing pencils in half, happy as J.P. Morgan.

Her classes have been packed to overflowing. As she guides the women through the steps, calling out encouragement, she tries to measure how much she'd miss them in France.

She and Craig spend the weekend together per usual. She doesn't mention Lyon and he doesn't ask and she's more confused than before.

She refills the glass of wine, settles into the armchair, and phones Mary Ellen for girl-to-girl advice.

"Fabulous!" Mary Ellen says. "After a year of this paramour business, I'd given up hope."

"I haven't decided yet."

"What more do you want, Anna?"

"We've been happy enough as we are."

"Shacking up on weekends is for college students. You can't do that forever."

She takes a long drink of wine. "But I don't know if I want to give up everything here for a year."

"You're getting this golden opportunity to see Europe. This may never come again."

She drinks more wine. Mary Ellen is sounding like Craig.

"I thought you enjoyed him."

"Yes, I do, but. . . ."

"Yes but, yes but. What the hell do you want, Anna?"

She raises the glass to her eyes and watches the burgundy lamplight undulate. "I want to save Humphrey."

"Who?"

"The whale in California who's swimming the wrong direction."

There's a silence at the other end. "I don't understand, Anna."

"Sorry. Let's talk about this some other time, okay?"

After they hang up, she pours a second glass of wine, or is it the third?

They used to understand each other. One could blurt out the craziest thought and the other one would say yes. Roommates; soul mates. But now they're like a radio that's drifted off center, so you hear two different stations at once.

In the bedroom she turns on the radio and Joni Mitchell's urgent voice grabs her. "The wind is in from Africa. Last night I couldn't sleep." Back in college she played the Blue album every day for weeks, months, until she'd memorized every syllable and every guitar scritch. "Oh, you're a mean old Daddy, but I like you." She walked across campus wanting to be strong and laugh along, looking for the key to set her free. Senior year, her friends aimed for law school or Wall Street. She was going to backpack through Europe to that village on the coast of Crete, where she'd drink red wine in the Mermaid Café and smash her empty glasses down.

But after graduation she first had to save enough money working crappy jobs. And then she fell in love with Al. Not enough money and too much Al. So here she sits in the middle of North Carolina. Landlocked. A hundred miles from the Carolina coast where she grew up with the throb of the ocean and the smell of salt beckoning through her bedroom window. Thousands of miles from Crete.

She lies on the bed, balancing the glass on her stomach. In Lyon she'd be a lot closer to Crete, but landlocked.

The phone rings. Two rings. Three. If it's Craig, she's not ready to talk.

"But what would you like to say to him?" Dr. Stern would ask if he were here, leaning forward. It was the interest that hooked her. Dr. Stern was so interested in her, wanted to know all about her. Unlike Al, who was afraid of knowing too much. Unlike Craig, who thinks he already knows everything. Dr.

Stern really listened to her and she couldn't wait to tell. All of it. She'd worked her way up to the moment she said goodbye to Al. She'd pictured him standing behind Dr. Stern and said: "I know I hurt you when I climbed into the passenger seat of Craig's car and went off with him. But I still want you to forgive me and let me go. Or if you can't forgive me, at least just let me go. And if you can't let me go, I'm going anyhow, because I'm a big girl now, a full-grown woman, and it's all right to leave home, even if you stood on the porch slump-shouldered as if I kicked you in the stomach. I didn't ask to be loved that much. Too much."

That was six months ago when, as Dr. Stern put it, "You've left a second time, but this time you understand why." It was the first praise she had earned from him. She repeated it to herself all week like a mantra. Understand why.

So why can't she figure out what to say to Craig?

She reads a page of *Joy Luck Club* and falls asleep with the light on.

· · ·

Her mind is sloshy from last night's wine, so she keeps losing her place in the newspaper. Midway through her third cup of coffee, she finds a little article. Yesterday Humphrey traveled 17 miles downriver, pursued by tugboats with underwater noisemakers and blinking lights. But since late this afternoon, the 45-ton whale has stalled at the Rio Vista Bridge, apparently frightened by the shadow of the girders.

She cocks her hip to nudge him under the bridge and down the river, out into the wide-open ocean where he belongs. But it's hopeless; he's frightened by shadows. One of these mornings she'll wake up and read he's dead.

. . .

Last night she'd spoken her statement aloud to her bathroom mirror again, getting the words right, getting to believe them. Now she faces him across the kitchen table. "I'm really touched, Craig. But I want to hold on to my life here."

His face closes. "Well, if that's the way you feel."

Silence. They dodge each other's eyes. She waits for him to lay out a counterargument, or for tears to fill his eyes—for something more than this limp silence. Finally she says: "I'm sorry."

"Me too. We could have had fun."

"Thanks for understanding."

"You're welcome." He gets to his feet. They hug for a long time, and he's gone.

The next morning she pulls on her leotard and feels wonderfully light, as if her legs were pumped full of air. She makes coffee. Hovers alongside the kitchen table, buttering the toast with wide sweeps.

When she unfurls the newspaper, there he is, on the front page. Humphrey, the wayward whale, glided into salt water yesterday after being lured by a device emitting underwater whale songs. A crowd of thousands lined the riverbanks to watch Humphrey pursue the small boat in which aquatic mammal researchers played tapes of humpback whales feeding.

She takes a sip of coffee. Goodbye, Humphrey. And what was it all about anyhow? First you chase some kind of death-wish upstream, then you chase a tape-recorded whale song downstream. Poor Humphrey. Now you're sending your song across the vast Pacific, swimming in widening circles until there's no doubt left: the singing whales have vanished and you're on your own.

She holds the toast at arm's length. What if she's too light? What if she leaves the house and the wind blows her into the path of a speeding car? Maybe she needs something to hold her down. The weight of a man upon her.

Something thick has lodged halfway down her throat.

She drops the toast in the trash. Shape up, Anna.

At the Body Shop she flips on the lights in the aerobics room, inserts the "Let's Get Physical" tape and sings along with Olivia Newton-John as she shines the mirrors.

Now that she's going to manage a second shop, she'll ask Todd for a raise, a hefty raise. And some day you'll find her on the coast of Crete, breathing in the wind from Africa, throwing down glasses of wine with a mean old daddy.

She puts on her leg-warmers and starts doing sit-ups. Soon her ladies will fill up the room with warbly greetings, waiting for her to make them limber and proud.

VENIAL SINS

On Tuesday afternoon during the third round of beers, revelation literally fell at my feet. One strip of color snapshots, that's all it was, but that was enough. Craig Mitchell, our man of the hour, had committed hanky panky with Anna Cox.

Until then it had been the usual promo party in honor of every newly-tenured professor of history. The same old guacamole and chips at the back table in Montezuma's Revenge. The same old joke: hey, Mitchell, now that you're an Assholesociate Professor you can use the faculty bathroom. Historians aren't exactly natural comedians, as any student will testify. Then again, students in the Reagan era are hardly amusing as they calculate their projected lifetime earnings down to the third decimal, like Ted Williams' batting average.

They don't even know who Ted Williams was. Wasn't he some kind of sports person back in your day, Professor Delaney? Back in my century is what you mean, you little bastard.

Craig Mitchell. Until that moment in Montezuma's Revenge, I thought I knew all about this fair-haired prince who was working his way toward some academic throne, preferably ivy-covered. Then those photos of him and Anna spilled out of his attaché case, whereupon I bent down and, after a momentary hesitation, slid them into my pocket. Who can fully decipher another man's motives, much less his own? I might say I intended to play Good Samaritan to my colleague Al Cox, alerting him to the misconduct of his long-legged, curvaceous wife. But the heat that crept across my face signaled a less virtuous motive: namely, the pleasure of confronting Mitchell with the evidence and watching him squirm.

It was like smoking. With every inhalation, I used to experience a tiny thrill, daring some cell to stage its cancer riot inside my lungs. With every exhalation I felt shame. Thrill and shame will keep you going forever, unless you have a loving wife like mine. I stopped smoking two days after my father died of lung cancer and Ellen threatened to kill me or divorce me or both if I didn't stop. She was watering the flowers in my study when she issued the threat, and before I could respond she was watering the pack of Luckies on my desk. Beneath the cigarettes my five freshly typed pages about Rousseau curled up in a wad. Ellen's gray eyes had turned near-black, which meant she was serious, and also beautiful, this clinical psychologist wife wielding a green watering can. "I'd like to have you around in my old age," she said.

Faced with that kind of love, of course I stopped smoking. Most of the time I forgive her my deprivation, except on those nights when I can't fall asleep because this smokeless, childless house seems unbearably lonely. I lie in bed and replay like an old baseball game those discussions about whether to keep on trying or adopt, try or adopt, a scoreless pitchers' duel that ended in our forties with us wearily saying we'll be just as happy after all without kids puking in our laps. So here we are, and really no one's to blame but God or Mother Nature. In bed with eyes closed, I imagine a mouthful of delicious nicotine and then breathe out my shame.

·   ·   ·

I hadn't disliked Mitchell at first. I actually felt sorry for him. There he stood in the doorway of my office, with neatly parted golden hair, rimless glasses, corduroy suit, and leather attaché case. "Excuse me. Craig Mitchell here, early modern Europe. I just want to say, Dr. Delaney, how much I admire your work on child-rearing among the nineteenth-century bourgeoisie. Ahead of its time, methodologically, although of course Braudel would say. . . ," all the while trying not to look up at the Renoir nude on the wall behind me.

I let him stand there jabbering until I remembered my own scared-shitless rookie year at UNC. "Glad to have you aboard the Titanic," I said, "and call me Vince." Whereupon he set down the attaché case, stepped around the pile of newspapers, and shook my hand. "I must tell you, Vince, they still remember you at Princeton."

Sure they do, Mitchell, just like you remember Ted Williams, who retired the year you got toilet-trained. But what I said was: "This isn't Princeton, but the bars are better here in Chapel Hill." He frowned and looked down at the attaché case as if for instructions, and finally shook my hand again with a brisk "thank you."

For a moment I felt sorry for Craig L. Mitchell—Andover, Yale B.A., Princeton Ph.D., winner of the Turner Prize, etc. etc.—who was contending with me and those luscious Renoir boobs. But what does feeling sorry get you other than a houseful of cats kicking kitty litter on the rug, and Ellen shouting, "No more cats! You promised me after number four. Find some other way to work out your needs." All right, I stopped taking in stray cats and I didn't try to woo Mitchell from his earnest upward path.

For the next three years, he and I discussed the weather and voted on opposite sides in faculty meetings and, during summer vacations, forgot each other entirely. Then one morning he asked me to critique his paper on "The French Family and Proto-industrialization," which he was going to deliver at the annual conference of the Society for Demographic and Family History, which would take place, Mitchell just happened to mention, in Florence.

"Florence, Italy?" I asked, just to keep things even.

He nodded, one hand holding out his paper.

"Do you want honest criticism," I asked, "or a few pats on the ass and corrections of typos?"

"Honest criticism, of course."

"Only a brave man or a fool asks for the truth."

"If you're too busy to read it, Vince, I certainly understand."

He looked young and hurt, like one of my Little Leaguers in the bottom of the ninth when I tell him to go back to the bench because I'm sending up a pinch hitter. "I'd be delighted," I said as I took the paper.

He shook my hand, of course, but he also did something that surprised me. Mitchell made a joke. Pointing up at the Renoir nude, who reclined between my old catcher's mitt and the photo of the St. Ignatius team (Regional Semifinalists, 1951), he said: "A rather unusual mascot, wasn't she?"

I laughed. A joke, maybe his first since kindergarten. Attaway to go, Mitch, and I slapped him on the butt like one of my Little Leaguers rounding third after hitting one over the fence.

For a moment I liked him, but it didn't last. How could it have lasted? Ridiculous. A slim young darling of the academic world, riding up his escalator of post-structuralist methodology, versus a fat old fart who keeps his stash of M&M's on the nightstand where the ashtray used to be and *still* coughs in the morning.

M&M's make me dream in color, I told Ellen when she complained about the crunching beside her.

She enjoyed that one. In fact she couldn't stop laughing, like back in the Sixties when we used to smoke dope in bed and laugh and make love to the beat of Creedence Clearwater Revival. We never dropped acid, although the Schafers kept urging us to join them. I have enough trouble living with the mind I have, thanks anyhow, friends. And of course there was that nasty chromosome question: Do you want a child looking like Timothy Leary? But the laugh turned out to be on us. The Schafers produced cuddly, beautiful Linda and Beth while we adopted Koshka, Snowball, Tramp, Mrs. Peacock and JJ. Why God wanted to make that tiny twist in Ellen's fallopian tube is, I suppose, one of those mysteries the Jesuits love to solve with those syllogisms I've long ago forgotten. But infertility is harder to forget.

From time to time I still wake up, drenched in sweat, from that dream of a baby wailing on the front porch while I run through room after room, around tables and chairs and over piles of newspapers, running as fast as I can, and when I finally open the door, the porch is empty. "What's wrong?" Ellen asks, propping herself on one elbow, and in the moonlight her hair is silver. "Nothing," I say. One night I dreamed Anna Cox stood naked beside my desk as I was typing, and she was holding a baby against her pale, magnificent breasts. What's wrong? Nothing.

. . .

Mitchell's paper was damn good. To be sure, it stuttered with jargon: "hegemonic" this and "hegemonic" that, plus too many "decennial cohorts." But it offered shrewd ideas about premodern family life and worked up to a bold hypothesis. At the end I questioned his definition of "middle class," explained how he could tighten the introduction, recommended an article on family structure in eighteenth-century Rouen, and wrote: *Well done, Mitch. Let's talk about it over a beer.* Slow straight pitches, right below the shoulders—no curves or screwballs.

"I'm really grateful, Vince," he said, tucking the manuscript into his attaché case, and I said "How about a few brews after work?" and he said "I'd love to, when I return," and off he trotted down the hall and away to Florence, Italy.

In the old days when I was younger, colleagues were collegial, gossiping in the halls, drinking awful coffee at the snack bar between classes. But now I walk to the men's room past all these closed office doors and I feel like a night watchman. Where is everyone? In the library or their study at home, I suppose, producing another book that twenty people in the world will read. Al Cox, for example. He and I used to drink margaritas at Montezuma's Revenge and debate whether Thoreau or Rousseau was more neurotic. But a few years ago he disappeared into the library stacks to finish his book—and into bed with his sexy young bride. Who can blame him, but still. . . .

These days, besides 115 undergraduates and five cats, I

have Ellen and Rousseau to keep me company. After Mitchell left, I started in again on my article about Jean-Jacques' childhood. At the age of seven, he accidentally tore his Latin book, whereupon his father locked him in the attic for three days. Each morning the boy received bread, water and a whipping.

A week later, Mitchell returned from Florence, Italy. "How was the conference?" I asked as we crossed paths in the faculty parking lot.

"Fabulous," he said, stepping into his shiny red Peugeot. "Your comments on my paper were really helpful, by the way."

"Let's get together for a beer."

"Next week would be good."

Two weeks later, Ellen and I were in the middle of a quiet evening of Scrabble à la Delaney (in French, four cents a point) and I was losing. I slammed my hand on the table, jostling the tiles.

"Don't try that trick," she said. "We're going to finish and you're going to pay."

"That smug little bastard!"

"You're not still obsessing about Mitchell, are you?"

"He can go off to Italy with my critiques but can't sit and have a beer with me. Who the hell does he think he is?"

"He's a smug little bastard and why can't you forget him?'

"A little gratitude: is that too much to want, sweetpea?"

She laughed. "You always want too much, darling."

Life proceeded, but in the post-Florence era I walked

around with a new twinge—very subtle, like a tiny torn ligament way down there in my chest. Too far down to diagnose. But every now and then, as I hunched over my desk writing and rewriting the effects of Père Rousseau's blithely abandoning his family in 1772 when Jean-Jacques was barely ten, that tiny ligament gave a tiny twitch and, holy shit, it hurt.

Envy? I asked myself: do you envy his hegemony? *Avarice?* Do you want an attaché case of your own? *Vanity? Sloth?* I went down that old venials list as smoothly as if I had been to Sunday school last week instead of forty years ago. *Gluttony? Lust?* And what's the seventh one, I asked myself in the mirror while I trimmed my beard? But all I knew was that I hurt.

Delaney hurt—now there's a magnificent insight for a scholar trained at St. Ignatius, Boston University and Princeton. Fifty years of life had come to this.

I combed my beard and grimaced. *Vanity*, was that the seventh? No, I'd already listed it. I hurt. Because of what he'd done to me. Or hadn't done. Not even a picture postcard of the Medici tombs. He went and came back locked up tight as an attaché case. Young Man Mitchell. Nobody's fool. One book published by Princeton, another in press, three articles, five reviews, not one fucking postcard.

. . .

Early Friday morning, Ellen went off with her sister to the mountains for five days, suffering her annual midwinter burnout from contending with a dozen emotionally disturbed adolescents. I hoisted her suitcase into the car and she gave me a long hug. "Water the plants on Sunday," she said, "Pay the phone bill, stay busy and," rubbing my crotch, "stay lonely. By Tuesday evening I'll be a decent person to live with again."

I stayed busy and lonely in a dozen ways. Watering the plants. Narrating the 1848 revolution to a roomful of less-than-thrilled students. Reading *Sports Illustrated* cover to cover at the dinner table while two cats purred in my lap. Finally getting Rousseau through his miserable childhood and sending him off to the *Journal of Interdisciplinary History*. Watching *Ordinary People* on the late-night movie channel and wondering how I would commit suicide if Ellen died first. Pills? Car? Razor? *Anger!* That was the seventh one.

At Mitchell's promo party on Tuesday afternoon, a rush of anger dizzied me as I leaned over to snatch that strip of colored photos from the floor of Montezuma's Revenge. Anna Cox? I gripped the edge of the table as I waited for my head to clear.

"What in hell are you and she up to?" I could have said to Mitchell. Or I could have flapped the photos against his cheek and, with a wink, murmured, "nice work!" But without a word I slipped them into my pocket and carried them home.

As I lay on the living-room couch beside watchful cats, the scotch and soda quieted the heart but fired up the brain. Mitch and Anna, the guilty couple, three times in a row. Here they are, cheek to cheek, blithe medley of red tie and green scarf. In the second frame, she sticks out her tongue and his face blurs with laughter. In the third frame their mouths meet, her silver earring gleams, his hand flies out of the picture. Kissing in a photo booth in an airport? In Florence? A week or year ago? They huddle like terrorists waiting for the explosions of light, get ready, now, and now, oh do it again, oh see how happy we are.

Ellen shook me awake as cats leaped to floor. "Hard day?" she asked. But that wasn't the question in her eyes as she glimpsed the photos.

"You don't want to know," I replied, shoving them into my pocket.

"Try me."

"Not yet." No need to make her an accessory to the crime. I'll clean this up by myself.

. . .

"Hey, Mitch, congratulations on the promotion." His desktop was vacant. The walls were bare. My voice echoed like a bad P.A. system inside his empty office, which he was moving out of because he was moving up to Trentholm's office. Assholesociate pushes out Emeritus: the cycle of history.

"Thanks, Vince." He stood up and smoothed the hair along his forehead. "Good of you to join the party yesterday."

"Wouldn't have missed it for the world," I said, fingering the photos in my pocket.

"Well, what can I do for you?" he asked, genial host,

seeming looser and larger than I remembered him, the rolling shoulders of an athlete, his eyes meeting mine carelessly.

"You dropped something yesterday." I pulled out the photos.

His eyebrows and glasses made a little bounce. "At Montezuma's Revenge?" Dismay, or maybe despair, crossed his face.

He reached for the photos but I stepped back. "Looks like you've been having some recreation between classes."

"Excuse me?"

"Getting tenure and getting laid in the same year. Congratulations."

"That's enough, Delaney." His eyes had turned ice-blue.

I waved the photos. "I once had a marvelous dream about Anna.

"Give me those and get out."

"But in reality, the closest I ever came was a hand on her ass one evening at the dean's party."

I smelled cologne as he leaned toward me. "Jesus, I thought even you had more style."

I wanted to drive my knuckles into his face. "How long have the two of you been fucking? And does Al Cox know? And who the hell do you think you are?"

He made a bitter smile. "What Anna and I did is our business, not yours or her former husband's." He took the photos from my hand. "They warned me you were eccentric, Delaney. But this time you've gone off the chart."

Former husband?

Mitchell strolled around the desk and opened the door. "Let's pretend this conversation never happened, shall we?"

I walked down the hall to my office, closed the door, and reached for the phone book. Cox, Albert, 114 Honeysuckle Drive. Cox, Anna, 5-A Colonial Apartments. There they were, living apart by one line, former husband above former wife, in plain view of everyone. Everyone except me.

The wooden chair creaked as I sat down. They warned him? Off the chart: was that really what they were thinking? Shame seeped through me.

I sat and the room turned dusky. Catcher's mitt. Renoir nude. Red scarf of some student who never came back. M&M's. A pile of newspapers. The photo of me and Ellen at Disney World. When did wanting become wanting too much?

I phoned Ellen to say I was grading papers and would be late.

"Something wrong?"

"I'll tell you tonight." First I needed to let the tumult of feelings subside.

I folded my hands upon the desk and watched the room turn dark.

I was going to tell her in bed after we made love, when we told each other everything. As we lay naked and a little breathless, I was about to say, "Do you remember Anna Cox?" But suddenly I was thinking of the sperm swimming madly upstream toward Ellen's womb and I had a craving for a cigarette. "Oh god," I began, but she interrupted, leaning over me to see the clock.

"In exactly forty-five seconds," she said, "we can congratulate ourselves."

"For what?" Her hair smelled of lilacs and sex.

"For managing to stay married twenty years, which is nineteen longer than the most optimistic predictions."

I had only forty-five seconds to make my confession, so instead of the anniversary I had forgotten or the photos I had stolen or the children I mourned, I chose to bunt. "I could have told you that," I said with a kiss.

She snuggled against me and whispered: "You've made me happy, Vince."

And because I loved her, I said: "You've made me happier than I deserve," which, I reminded myself, was also true.

THE RELICS OF VINCE DELANEY

She sat in darkness and listened for his footsteps on the porch, as if he were merely late. As if he were about to come down the hall shouting "Guess who's home and voracious," with the cats meowing at his feet. As if yesterday the policeman hadn't knocked gently on the door.

She pressed a hand against her mouth. Her gold ring was bitter-tasting.

Why didn't she cry? She wanted to cry, but her jaw was clenched tight. Throbs of pain climbed into her eyes. If he were here, he would rub her head while he recounted the chairman's latest idiocy, until soon he'd become too agitated and rub too hard. "Stop," she'd say, "you're only making it worse."

It was so hot. When she lifted the hair away from her

neck, her body smelled dank. The windows were wide open but the air hung thick as cotton. What was she supposed to do with herself? Maybe she shouldn't have told everyone to stay away—no tears, no casseroles.

She went to the kitchen and sat in front of the wilting salad she had made hours ago. During dinner he liked to ask about her clients: the boy who talked to sheep; the rock guitarist afraid of crossing bridges. Sometimes he forgot to eat, planting elbows on either side of his plate, tugging at his beard. "Dreamed of a shark in his bathtub? I bet you a dollar this kid has a domineering mother." He waved his fork, spraying rice on the rug. "What do you think? Good enough for the *Journal of Family Therapy*?"

"It would be better if you didn't throw your food." That would set him laughing, his squeaky laugh. . . .

She jumped as a motorcycle roared past the window.

Mealtime therapy and Scrabble were their best games. Scrabble à la Delaney: he owed her $1,042. "And sex," he would have said. "How interesting, you always 'forget' to list sex," he would have said, scratching his balls, delighted with himself.

She remembered sex. She remembered everything. His hand on her cheek when she wakened from a bad dream. How he gathered cats, one or two under each arm, en route to the breakfast table. Eating birthday cake in bed.

She gave a little moan. Dead. He was dead. "Dead," she said aloud in the dark. "How can you be dead?"

Even reading this morning's paper didn't make it make sense. *Vincent J. Delaney, professor of French history at the University since 1964, died yesterday at the age of 52 from a traumatic concussion by riding a neighbor boy's tricycle. According to patrolman Ernie Blake, "Apparently the Professor was traveling downhill at a high rate of speed when he lost control at the intersection of Honeysuckle and Shadylawn Roads and capsized against the pavement." Nobody at the Delaney home was available to explain why he was riding the tricycle. Four-year-old Jimmy Eubanks said he was home watching TV when his tricycle was wrecked.*

If only she'd been looking out the window instead of making gazpacho. She'd have seen him set his briefcase on the sidewalk, recognized the grin that signaled one of his pranks, and she could have chased him as he whooped and swerved downhill and caught him before. . . .

"You son of a bitch." She threw the salad across the room and the cats scattered. Gone, with no warning. Forever. On a stupid tricycle. Leaving her here alone. "How could you, Vince?" Tears were seeping between her fingers, more and more of them, and she sagged gratefully against the back of the chair.

It had been years she'd called him Vince. *If you overuse a word*, he believed, *you wear out its meaning.* That's why they called each other by nicknames: Sweetpea; Okra; Dr. D. and Humbum. Their friends thought it charming, except their feminist friends, who found it appalling. Nobody understood they were preserving themselves for each other.

Snowball rubbed against her ankle. She scooped him into her lap, where he settled with a rhythmic purr.

What would they have done if they'd had a child? Would they have inscribed a name upon the birth certificate and never used it? He wanted a child riding on his shoulders as he galloped down the hall—a child whose lunch box he'd fill with M&M's when she wasn't looking; who would make them a true family when they visited Disney World. He didn't need to confess it to her; she knew, from the silence with which he greeted the results of those tests they—she—had failed. "I'm sorry, Okra," she'd said that rainy afternoon as they drove home from the hospital. "We'll adopt."

He shook his head as he drove at half his usual speed, turning each corner carefully as if she were ill. "Now we'll have us all too ourselves," he said in thickened voice, peering through the wet windshield. She was shocked by the gladness blooming in her chest. She hadn't really wanted children, only him.

It was almost midnight and she was desperately tired. She'd clean up this mess tomorrow.

. . .

The next afternoon, her sister arrived from Asheville in a brand-new Buick. "How are you, sweetie?" Lucinda said, enveloping here in a hug.

"I've been better."

"Well, I took sick leave at the store, and I didn't want to go to that board meeting at the church. So I'll stay as long as you need me."

"Thanks," she said. And then with more emphasis, more warmth: "That's good of you, Lucinda." But already she felt a twinge of being taken over instead of taken care of. Widow.

Lucinda had brought Tupperware bowls filled with baked ham, succotash, and potato salad; neatly written condolences from her three girls; a bunch of gladiolas Carl had picked himself; and a large plaid suitcase. After taking it all inside, they drank iced tea and chatted about the girls and potato salad recipes just like they did at their last get-together and the one before that—amiable topics to carry them through a weekend without anger or tears or any such honest messiness. Of course, considering the history between her sister and Vince, maybe recipes were preferable to honesty. Still, you'd think death might make a difference.

"Ellen? Did you hear what I said?"

She stood up. "Let's get some air."

They drove to the botanical garden and walked single-file along the winding trail, reciting the Latin names on the metal tags. It was nearly dark when they drove up to the house. Lucinda pulled the handbrake but didn't turn off the motor. "What will you do with yourself now?"

"I'll work. And grocery shop. And feed his damn cats. And hope I'm exhausted enough to sleep."

"Living alone—I can't imagine it—such a hardship, but

on the other hand he could be a handful of trouble, couldn't he. I mean that in the nicest way, of course."

She hesitated, just for a moment, and then decided to say what he would say if he were here. "No, you don't. You disapproved of him from the start. Sure, he wasn't nice to you, or sometimes even to me, but he was . . ." her hand groped for the right words, "bigger than that."

"I was just looking out for you."

Always the big sister, she almost said as she unbuckled her seat belt and fumbled for the door handle. It was hopeless. Whenever they tried talking about Vince they ended up circling each other like hissing cats. In the dusk, in Lucinda and Carl's brand-new Buick, she couldn't find the goddamn door handle.

"Here." Lucinda reached across her lap and slid a little lever.

"I don't need help," Ellen said more fiercely than she'd expected. But she left the words there, unapologized for. Widows could get away with being rude, at least for a while. Long enough to defend themselves.

As she set the table for dinner, she made up her mind to ask her sister, politely, to leave in the morning. She needed to think about Vince. And she couldn't do that in the company of Lucinda, who had disliked him ever since the rehearsal dinner the evening before their wedding. Much wine had been drunk by the time Lucinda raised her glass and said: "I wish for you the same love and happiness that Carl and I have enjoyed every day of our marriage. Our recipe is simple: first thing in the morning, kiss each other and say I love you."

"Ah, Lucinda," he said, rising to his feet. "Now you've got me worried. As your sister will testify, until I've had two cups of coffee I'm grumpy as hell."

Ellen tugged on his arm but he wouldn't be deterred. "Of course a little whoopee would perk me up, but morning breath is hardly conducive to sex. Alas, our marriage will never match yours and Carl's."

"Damn it," she hissed as he sat down, "you've spoiled everything," even as she felt a tickle of laughter inside her chest.

While the guests gazed down into their filets mignon, Lucinda huffed to the ladies' room and Carl told Ellen that only a southern sense of family loyalty restrained him from punching out his future brother-in-law. She promised that Vince would apologize, and he did. Throughout the evening and well into the next afternoon, in fact, he offered increasingly elaborate apologies, outlining his various neuroses, recounting his adolescent rebellion against Jesuit teachers, buying a corsage for Lucinda, his mother-in-law, even Carl. But it was too late; the wedding had turned into some sort of melodrama.

"At least it wasn't boring," he said that night in bed.

"Is that the best you can say after embarrassing me and making everyone angry?"

"No." He put his hands on either side of her face and

kissed her eyelids. "The best I can say is I love you. And," he added, "I promise we'll have a marriage you'll never forget."

In the morning she explained to Lucinda how grateful she was for everything but she needed to be alone, just for a while, just long enough to get herself straightened out.

All day she listened again and again to Bach's B-Minor Mass, which was the longest, saddest piece of music they owned, and fed the cats and ate cottage cheese on crackers, and didn't answer the phone. Gradually she stopped thinking of anything except the choral voices. Her body seemed to fit more snugly around her. She felt more content in this house by herself.

. . .

The funeral disposed of his body but not the sudden, omnivorous desolation that ambushed her in the supermarket aisle or at a green light. One day she realized, with horns blaring around her, that she'd swerved across two lanes of traffic. She could fend off the grief during the day while she counseled her troubled adolescents, but it swooped back at dinnertime. Cats had no interest in her stories.

Clearing out his clothes helped. Without the tweed jackets and rumpled blue shirts and baseball caps, the closet no longer taunted her every morning with the notion that maybe, just maybe, he had walked down the driveway in his pajamas for the newspaper. Well then, keep clearing out. On Saturday afternoon she took three large boxes and drove to his office: one box for personal mementos, one for the Thrift Shop, and the last for the dumpster.

Prof. Delaney, Knock and Enter, the sign on the door commanded in his familiar blue scrawl. Her hand trembled as she fitted the key into the lock. The air inside the office was stale, lifeless, but he was all over the place, as if he'd just strolled down to the men's room to pee. On the wall, the poster of the pink, sumptuous Renoir nude, who gazed disconcertingly at visitors, which is exactly why he hung it there. And over here the catcher's mitt, souvenir of that glorious high school championship game he would narrate, inning by inning, if you weren't careful. The leather was split by a hundred tiny lines. She put her face against the well and smelled, faintly, something that was less leather than sweat.

A little tremor went through her. Maybe this was too soon.

Get on with it, she told herself. A shoelace lay on the floor beside piles of *The New York Times* and index cards scribbled upon in French, illegible French, and the red pillow she'd embroidered for him one Christmas with the face of a cat. On his desk, the photo of the two of them smiling arm in arm at Disney World leaned against a cup of brown liquid crusted by milky green mold. Alongside it were a dozen well-chewed pencils, three half-empty bags of M&M's, a box of toothpicks (how many forms of orality can one man find?) plus a copy of the *American Historical Review*. In the typewriter a sheet of paper was blank except for a half-sentence: *If the truth be known, by the time Rousseau neared middle age he felt impossibly. . .*

She wasn't ready for this. A Vincent Delaney museum. A mausoleum.

The middle drawer of the desk wouldn't open and then, with a shudder, it did, revealing more flotsam and jetsam, but also something gleaming in the back corner: a gold hoop earring. She cupped it in her palm. On her thirtieth birthday he'd given her earrings far more expensive than an assistant professor could afford. Fourteen-carat gold, with platinum wires. That night, after a four-course dinner at La Residence and before making love, she reached up to one earlobe and felt nothing but smooth skin. "We'll never find it," she wailed.

"Wear only one, then."

"No, I'd always think of the loss." She took out the survivor and laid it in his palm. "Keep this for me in case the other one turns up."

He was never coming home. Not today. Not ever. She set down the earring and fumbled in her pocket for a tissue to dry the tears. All too often he'd disappointed her, outraged, irked or appalled her, but never forsaken her. Whatever else, never that.

God knows, though, he'd teetered on the brink. That evening with Anna Cox, for instance. Anna Cox, former student and fresh wife of Albert Cox, years younger than everyone else at that faculty cocktail party, masking her anxiety behind wide blue eyes that could be read to say anything anyone wanted to believe. Slim, high-breasted Anna, wearing a short white dress and dangling silver earrings, who seemed unaware of the electricity she showered on everything male.

Ellen recognized the type. But if she did, why didn't— or wouldn't—Vince, who prided himself on seeing through every sham? She watched from across the room as he chatted warmly with Anna. Poured her a glass of wine and laughed with her. And in the kitchen where he had gone to refill his plate with oysters, where he could believe he was out of sight, he cupped one hand against the smooth curve of Anna's right buttock.

Ellen had felt a surge of fury. She leaned dizzily against the wall. "Are you having fun?" she asked when he returned.

"Fun?" Wine slopped out of his glass as he gestured toward the room. "You know I hate these academic shindigs."

"Liar." She turned, walked away, fast, and didn't look back.

Halfway down the driveway he caught up with her, breathing hard. "Jesus! What's going on?"

"I'm not going to play the patient forgiving wife while you sneak around with Anna and . . . and. . . ." She couldn't finish it.

He took her in his arms. His belly pushed against her. His breath smelled of wine. "Don't be absurd, Ellen. You're my everything."

She stroked the dark grain of the desktop inscribed with

years of overfull coffee cups (cream and too much sugar), careless cigarettes, and over here at the edge, what looked like a shakily etched heart. He'd carried this desk from college dorm to grad student apartment to faculty office. His belongings and his body had outgrown it, but of course he wouldn't think of parting with it. "This desk knows me too well," he said. It had survived her outburst years ago when she'd watered his pack of cigarettes, along with the Rousseau manuscript and everything else, and ordered him to stop smoking or else.

She'd saved him from lung cancer but couldn't save him from an idiotic tricycle.

If the truth be known, by the time Rousseau neared middle age he felt impossibly. . . . As last wills and testaments go, at least for professors tricycling to their deaths, this one was pretty good. Damn good. After all, it left the punch line up to her, didn't it?

She put the earring into her ear. Then she phoned the campus police. "This is the widow of Professor Vincent Delaney. I need some help. If you happen to have a couple of strong men who are free for an hour. . . ."

She had no idea how long she waited. At one point she opened the window, and a breeze worked among the papers on the desk. Sometime later, she pulled open the large bottom drawer, swept one arm along the desktop, and watched everything topple in. Then she added the catcher's mitt. As for the rest, she'd come back some other day.

The two black men were large and taciturn and extremely

courteous. They tiptoed among the junk and took positions facing each other across the desk. With a nod, they picked it up. Things rattled inside and the men looked toward her. "It's all right," she said. Down the hall they went with small deliberate steps, the muscles in their arms and necks pushing out sharply, but they didn't hurry or speak a word. At the elevator they set it down. When the door opened, they lifted it again.

She gave them the address and drove behind their pickup truck in first gear, never more than ten miles an hour, slower around the corner on Franklin Street, slower yet down Curtis and up Honeysuckle. The desk didn't move an inch, so far as she could see, and she kept her eyes on it through the entire journey.

The men carried it across the yard, across the living room, and finally set it beside the other desk in Vince's study, rubbing their forearms along their sweaty faces, pocketing the money with a nod, softly closing the front door behind them.

The cats crept out of hiding, sniffed the desk, rubbed against its legs, making little noises in their throats.

There was barely room to stand and none to vacuum. "It's all right," she said. "There's more of you at home now."

THE REAL WORK OF THE DAY

"Good morning, Mr. Weber."

"Not yet, Marie." He grunted as he bent down and stowed his lunch bag in the little refrigerator behind her desk. "My taxi wasn't air-conditioned."

"Neither was my subway."

"*Touché.* I'll pay for your taxi home."

Safely inside his office, he closed the door. Ash-gray light seeped in from the airshaft. He removed his jacket, his tie, his sweated-through white shirt, and pulled from the briefcase a fresh white shirt. For a moment he thought of not putting it on, but he did, slowly, and knotted the tie an inch below his Adam's apple (a compromise between executive perfection and breathing).

Eighty-two degrees out there, according to the thermometer on the windowsill. Another New York City record loomed. He settled into his chair, switched on the computer and listened to it awakening with gurgles and beeps. Like Alice, yes, sounding just like Alice in her crib eighteen years ago. He and Harriet would lie in each other's arms listening to their daughter in the next room as she came awake like a small forest of birds. Eighteen years later, here he sat, editor-in-chief of *The Almanac of Has-Beens*, wondering, as he did almost every morning, whether this would be the day he quit.

He double-clicked and frowned at the reply he'd been struggling to write to Carlton Branch in Champaign, Illinois. *Dear Mr. Branch. Although I am impressed [awed?] by your accomplishment [feat?] of reading the entire New Testament aloud on your cable TV station, I regret—I must regretfully explain. . . .*

Carlton Branch was another of the thousands who mistook his purposes. The *Almanac* didn't seek the biggest, the farthest, the youngest or oldest, the most something in the shortest time. Leave all that to the *Guinness Book of World Records*. He commemorated those who had once been famous, or else notorious, or at least quixotic, and were now forgotten. "Although history immortalizes the winners," he'd declared in the preface to last year's *Almanac*, "let us not forget the also-rans." It was uphill preaching. In the age of boomboxes, no one heard anybody else.

"I'm thinking of quitting," he'd told Harriet last night while they made dinner.

"Again, Chaz?" She was stirring the spaghetti sauce. "Have you finished the salad?"

"Almost. But this time I mean it. I'll go back to work at a trade publishing house."

She kept stirring and her hips stirred in cadence. Standing there in bare feet and denim skirt, with light brown hair flowing down her back, she could almost have been twenty-one, the girl who was whistling *Rhapsody in Blue* while she walked her cat across the Carolina campus that Sunday morning in 1968. The girl whom he had followed back to her dorm. But her hair was streaked with gray now, and she'd put on weight here and there. In the mornings she clicked off to work in high heels.

He snapped a celery stalk. "Health benefits. Pension plan. Why should I be ashamed to want that?"

"You'll feel better tomorrow after your check-up."

"Don't humor me, Harriet."

"You used to like being humored." She licked the wooden spoon. "Especially the way I tickled your funny bone, remember?"

He nodded, shrugged. "Is the spaghetti done yet?"

She started to say something but didn't. She plucked a spaghetti strand from the pot, held it steaming in mid-air, and flung it against the wall. "Done."

The wall resembled a washed-out Jackson Pollock canvas,

bearing the grayish traces of all the spaghetti dinners of their marriage. Last Christmas he'd bought her a windup egg timer, but she swore by her French grandmother's method and said no thanks. That's how they did it these days. He said his piece and she said hers and then they went on about their lives. Not like the early days, when they used to really take each other on.

Dear Mr. Branch. Although I am impressed [awed?] by your. . . . He wound the egg timer. Five minutes to finish this letter and then he'd start on the real work of the day.

"For god's sake, Weber," Flannery had exclaimed, "why don't you just Xerox a goddamn little rejection letter for these crackpots?" But he remembered opening those self-addressed manila envelopes fifteen—no, twenty—years ago, and pulling out his novella with a printed message clipped to the corner: *We regret that this material does not suit our needs. The Editors.* Not a single hand-written word, not a hair or fingerprint or coffee-cup stain. The novella that began with the crash and fiery death of a man and woman whose three-year-old son Francis was deposited with a bewildered aunt who take care of him about as well as an aunt could. . . . None of this heart-stirring story had elicited one personal word from The Editors, who surely were themselves sons or daughters.

The timer rang. *But your extraordinary achievement, Mr. Branch, is more appropriate for* The Guinness Book of World Records.

Eighty-six degrees out there. By lunchtime this would

become the thirty-fifth day above ninety, five days short of a record. The air hung motionless upon the city—rancid, adhering to one's eyelids, like a vast bus exhaust. On Saturday a man was found in an alley, dying of heat stroke. Joggers were warned not to jog; the fat, the old and the ill were told to stay home.

He pressed a hand against his chest. He should go on his diet again, tell Harriet to rid the apartment of starch and fats and sugar, as they'd done in 1974, their thin year, when they celebrated Nixon's resignation by joining a ballroom dancing class and dieting. Wednesday nights they glided across the Millard Fillmore Junior High gymnasium as the waltzes and tangos poured out of the record player and Miss Zambrella chanted "one and one-two-three." Sergeant Zambrella, he and Harriet called her, limping home to the baby sitter and a hot bath. But every Wednesday they felt a little lighter, a little more grateful, until there they were, hand in hand beneath the basketball hoop, being awarded second prize in the under-forty tango competition.

A sour bubble of gas popped in his throat. He reached into the desk drawer for the Alka Seltzer. "Marie," he murmured over the intercom, "would you please bring me a glass of water and the Wilcox file?" Two weeks he'd been trying to complete that essay. Today, surely today!

Ella Wheeler Wilcox (Nov. 5, 1850—Oct. 30, 1919), the most popular poet of her time. Author of the scandalous *Poems of Passion* (1883). Prolific versifier as well as syndicated columnist in Hearst newspapers. "A pure thoroughbred lowbrow," to quote her (only) biographer. Who couldn't recite those opening lines of "Solitude"? *Laugh, and the world laughs with you;/Weep, and you weep alone.* On the other hand, who but Charles Weber, author of a senior honors thesis on Diderot's encyclopedia could recognize Ella Wheeler Wilcox's name today?

After six months of intense labor under Professor Delaney, he had graduated with highest honors and was driving a U-haul truck north with Harriet and all their belongings—a freshly married Bachelor of Arts, eager to astonish the New York literary world with the novel he had in mind. He wrote every morning and afternoon on the kitchen table and stacked groceries on the A&P shelves at night while Harriet catalogued at the New York Public Library until finally the novel was done and their debts were scarily high and she was pregnant.

"Are you feeling all right, Mr. Weber?"

Marie reminded him of Alice, which is why he'd hired her. Not merely the auburn hair framing her narrow face. It was the way she spoke, in soft unhurried phrases, as if she understood things—him. Her slender hands were holding out a glass of water like a bouquet.

"Just a bit of heartburn, Marie."

Nothing had prepared him for that first encounter with his daughter. As her furry head rested in the saucer of his palm and she scrutinized him with large eyes, all at once he felt claimed. A finger pointing straight into his heart. She was his for life . . . although on September 2nd, before he was prepared, she would be going away to college. "Providence isn't far, Dad." It might as well be Africa. "Oh, Chaz," Harriet said, "you'll get used to her being gone." That's what they'd been telling him all his life, and he still wasn't used to anyone being gone.

"Do you want anything else, Mr. Weber?" Marie handed him the manila folder.

"I want a ticket on the Kon Tiki, drifting across the Pacific under a cool breeze."

She smiled tenuously (too young to remember Thor Heyerdahl, he realized too late) and then she left him alone with Ella Wheeler Wilcox.

> *How does Love speak?*
> *In the wild words that uttered seem so weak*
> *They shrink ashamed to silence; . . . in the warm*
> *Impassioned tide that sweeps through throbbing veins,*
> *Between the shores of keen delight and pains. . . .*

There was more throbbing here than Victorian Americans were used to. Ministers and literary critics ganged up on this unladylike poetess, chastising her for out-Whitmaning Whitman and out-Swinburning Swinburne, which of course immediately fanned the fire. Before she could catch her breath, *Poems of Passion* sold sixty thousand copies and her reputation was made. To look at her photograph, though, you would hardly think Miss Wheeler a scandalous woman. The scoop-necked taffeta dress flowed to the floor, muffling the curves of her heavy-set body. Dark hair was piled high above a sharp-chinned, long-nosed face. With gloved hands folded at her waist, she gazed solemnly toward the public whom her words had inflamed. At heart she remained the Wisconsin farm girl who wrote quatrains about unending love, tides of woe, and God's arching skies above. Surely it was not immoral, she protested, to voice the longings of one's soul.

His fingers jumped from the keyboard when the phone buzzed. "It's your wife on line one," Marie said.

He tucked the phone against his cheek, nursing a twinge of alarm. She usually called after lunch, not before. "Are you all right, Har?"

"Of course. But what did he say about you?"

"He?"

"The doctor. Oh Chaz, you didn't miss your appointment again, did you?"

Had he? For the second time? How obvious could one be! He squinted at the calendar. "One-fifteen. The appointment's at 1:15, Harriet. So there!"

"But you had forgotten, hadn't you?"

"Let's say I had two hours left to remember."

"The almanac man who can't remember his own annual check-up. Pretty funny."

Not in the slightest, and neither of them laughed. "Don't worry, Har. Everything'll turn out fine. Bye."

As if she were the one who was worried about whatever Dr. Merriman might find lurking inside him. There was no lump or bleeding, no particular pain. But ever since Aunt Luce had died, his body had become strange. His flesh seemed to have loosened at the arms and belly, like the stuffing in his childhood teddy bear. He ate in spurts, pot roast and gravy and rolls, followed by a day of nothing. He slept raggedly, waking up in a sweat at dawn, his heart drumming madly.

> *Lust is the hot simoon whose burning breath*
> *Sweeps o'er the fields with devastating death.*

Simoon: a hot dry violent wind laden with dust from Asian and African deserts. *Lust* . . . but no one needed a dictionary for that. With *Poems of Passion,* Ella Wheeler became a household name. The fact was, however, that at the age of thirty-three she hadn't yet touched first-hand either love or death. Both would happen soon enough.

For weeks she had been receiving letters from Robert Wilcox, a silver-company executive who had glimpsed her at a jewelry store, learned her name, and felt impelled to write. The letters were witty, intelligent, warm but not sentimental, each arriving in an envelope of luminous blue. He told her about his travels through Russia, about the Gautier novel he was reading, about being orphaned at an early age. Repeatedly he asked to meet, until at last she consented to dine with him in a fancy Chicago hotel. He was in person all that his letters had promised, and more. When she learned that Mr. Wilcox was, like herself, a believer in spiritualism and reincarnation, she made up her mind. Within a year, they were married. Three years later, a son was born and—

There was a knock at the door, then Marie's face peeked in. "I'm going to lunch now. Do you want to take the phone, since Mr. Flannery's on vacation, or should I turn on the answer machine?"

The dilemma of a three-person staff. The title of editor-in-chief was a little masquerade he played against the world out there.

"The answer machine, please."

No interruptions. Tuna fish sandwich at the desk. He should have finished Ella Wheeler Wilcox by now and started on Robert Scott. But in this kind of weather it was hard to imagine dying inside an ice-crusted tent near the South Pole.

In the refrigerator behind Marie's desk his lunch bag was leaning against the bottle of champagne left over from his forty-fifth birthday party—the surprise party that Marie, Harriet and Alice had conspired to pull off. He'd opened the door to find balloons from floor to ceiling, forty-five balloons and one to grow on. The first and only surprise birthday party in his life. With tears in his eyes, he'd hugged everyone, even Flannery.

Three years later, their son was born and died within a few hours. A malformation of the heart, the doctor explained. Incurable, tragic. For the rest of their lives, the Wilcoxes would be left with each other, which was surely a great happiness but always achingly incomplete, like the shoulder's memory of an amputated arm. So they sought to contact their son. They consulted Swami Vivekananda in New York, psychics in California and Paris, a Hindu astrologer in Cairo, a ouija board at home in their parlor, whoever and whatever. Silence, nothing but silence from the beyond. Yet they kept hoping.

A drop of mayonnaise glistened on the spacebar. He wiped it away with a Kleenex.

"I'm back, Mr. Weber."

One o'clock. He went down to the hall to the men's room and brushed his teeth, although come to think of it, Dr. Merriman wasn't a dentist.

. . .

"Well, Charlie, you're a perfectly healthy forty-five-year-old male, except for twenty pounds around the middle." Dr. Merriman clapped him on the shoulder with the same hand that had been tapping and squeezing and probing his body for the past hour.

Charles bent to tie his shoes. "Good news."

"What did you expect?"

"I don't know." His fingers couldn't control the laces. If he was perfectly healthy, why wasn't he feeling well?

"Go easy on the beer, Charlie. Jog twice a week, have sex every night, and I bet you'll live to ninety."

The blood was running into his head so he couldn't see the laces. He straightened up. "Just what the hell makes you think I want to live to ninety?"

Dr. Merriman tugged at the stethoscope around his neck. "Hey, friend, lighten up."

"No teeth, half-blind, wetting the bed at night. No thanks." He walked out of the office.

When Aunt Luce was taken to the nursing home at the age of eighty-four, he had cleared out her little apartment. The job was more than he'd bargained for—like visiting Pompeii after the volcano. A dusty *Reader's Digest* lay open on the couch. Three bananas rotted in a soft black mound. Beside the bed were the dusty photos of himself as child, teenager and man. Most poignant, for some reason, were the fifteen empty mayonnaise jars lined up in two rows in the kitchen cabinet, sparkling clean, waiting to perform some duty that never came. He threw them into the Dempsey Dumpster along with the rest of the goods Aunt Luce had assembled against the future. The weight of a lifetime had settled into those three rooms. It gave him a backache he needed a week to recover from.

Aunt Luce, once installed between the metal bars of her new bed, took ten months to die, losing a few pounds and then a few more, becoming smaller each time he visited. He looked down at her wide-eyed, bony head perched atop that dwindling body and he couldn't stop himself from thinking of the fetus he'd seen in Harriet's pregnancy book as they waited for Alice to clamber into their lives. One hot night in July, during the seventh inning of the All Star Game, the phone rang and he turned down the sound on the TV. It was the hospital; his aunt had died an hour ago. He remembered the outfielders racing silently across the grass, the fans rising with outstretched hands and upturned faces, opening their mouths in silence, while the voice said in his ear, "I'm very sorry."

He stepped out of the lobby and plunged into the heat. It hovered between the buildings, shuddered up from subway grates. He stood on the corner and waved at taxicabs until his shirt clung to his skin and he was breathing in little gasps. He didn't want to collapse here on Lexington Avenue, staring up at the faces of strangers. Finally a cab screeched to a halt and he was saved for another day.

· · ·

His parents' car had driven at high speed head-on into a pickup truck that had drunkenly crossed the median. They were killed instantly, although the fire burned around them for thirty minutes. The police and firemen arrived first. The ambulance arrived and, unneeded, drove away. It was almost midnight when the New Jersey Highway Patrol phoned the babysitter. She had fallen asleep in front of the TV, so it took a while for her to understand what the officer was trying to explain. Charlie slept in the next room in the yellow glow of the Donald Duck night-light. He slept through that phone call and the ones to the babysitter's parents and to Aunt Luce. He slept through the night. When he woke up in the morning, he found Aunt Luce in place of his mother and father. She poured his cereal and said they'd been delayed. Later, as she spread her sheets on their bed, she said in a choked voice that they'd had an accident. Eventually, after he stopped waking up at night wailing, she said they wouldn't be back.

One afternoon in high school, he had turned the brittle pages of the *Star-Tribune* and found the story—the truck, the fire, and so forth—but the details made surprisingly little difference. They explained how his parents disappeared but added nothing to their absence. He had salvaged a few phrases ("time for beddy-bye, Charlie boy"), the strength of his mother's arms around him, the sweetish smell of his father's pipe. And of course that five-by-seven snapshot. He is standing knee-deep in snow, his round face wreathed by a furry hood, his lower lip between his teeth. His mother holds his right hand and looks down upon him as if he were a gift that had just been delivered. On his left, his father holds a pipe out toward the horizon. Snapshot and pipe smell and a phrase or two: flimsy items. By now he might be remembering his memory of them. He'd lived one quick life and then one morning woke up to start a new one.

. . .

After thirty-two years of unwavering devotion, Robert Wilcox—"this rare soul," as she called him—died of pneumonia. Ella felt "shipwrecked." She took daily doses of morphine. How could she survive without the other half of her life? But he was not gone. One cool September evening as she sat in her parlor, the pointer on the ouija board began swiveling rapidly, urgently, with his astral message. "Time is naught; hope for bliss with me; I am incomplete without you." And then came, at long last, the news that he had met their son. "How did you recognize him?" she asked. "He was so like you," the pointer spelled out in reply.

During her last years, she bleached her hair and wore a dress pulled low over her plump breasts. She carried an armful of daffodils. "It is a curious thing how the body and mind react one on the other," she told her readers. "If you sit and smile before the mirror for ten minutes, you will soon feel your heart growing merry." When the pain grew unbearable, however, she withdrew to her bedroom and, at the end of nine months of suffering, died of cancer. "She was," the *Philadelphia Record* declared, "an inspiration of strength and comfort to the many who looked upon her as the foremost writer of her time." But she cared less about what she left behind than whom she was going to rejoin.

He picked up the phone and dialed the familiar number. "Hello, Harriet? The doc said I'm fit as a fiddle. Going to live to ninety, he told me. I think I'll go home early."

On the way, he stopped at his favorite bakery and bought a chocolate cake.

. . .

A pile of mail huddled against the door: gas bill, electric bill, Chinese restaurant takeout menu, and the Carolina

Alumni Review. Inside, the apartment was hushed except for the rattle of the refrigerator. Alice must have been holding it open for ten minutes while she pondered ice cream flavors. On hot afternoons, she ate a bowl of ice cream because it helped homework go faster. He crossed the living room toward her room, smiling, and then he remembered she was gone. Three weeks hiking somewhere in the Rockies. Outward bound. And on to Providence in September. His precious cargo, launched into the unmapped future. He leaned his forehead against her door. *Providence isn't far, Dad.* But it wasn't home, it damn sure wasn't home.

He stepped into her room. The air was musty, preserved. Sunlight burned through the Venetian blinds, inscribing thin white stripes on the blue bedspread. The poster of Monet's lily pond covered half the wall, tilting slightly down toward the left. He'd thumbtacked it here after one of their Sunday outings to the museum. "Now I can lie in bed and float across it with my eyes," she said. She'd been nine, ten at most, and when she stood on tiptoe and folded her arms around his neck to kiss him, he'd held onto her, head bent against the pillow of her auburn hair. Her skinny body wiggled within his arms, as if they were dancing. A few years later, she'd taped beside Monet's lily pond the glossy magazine photo of this man—this "absolute hunk"—reclining in his bulging Calvin Klein underpants. As if her father needed to be punched in the eye to understand she was growing up. Growing breasts. Goodbye. He had begun saying goodbye long ago, ever since he was three years old.

A cold drink, that's what he needed. He sat at the kitchen table with a glass of lemonade, leafing through the *Alumni Review*. *Vincent Delaney, renowned historian, dies at age 52.* No! Impossible! Not Prof. Delaney. Who would have guessed that he was only seven years older than Charles himself? The prof had seemed middle-aged: not just the potbelly, but the aura of sad knowledge he carried into the classroom. But when the bell rang, he came alive, bigger than life, gesticulating in a rumpled blue shirt, dark half-moons under the armpits, filling the classroom with the Jacobin reign of terror, Rousseau, French expletives. Charles was so enthralled by the lectures that he forgot to take notes. *After 24 years at UNC, he suffered a fatal concussion in an accident outside his home.* Did he fall from the roof as he swept off leaves? Or have a stroke? Gone. Ever since that conversation in senior year, he'd promised himself to write a letter thanking the professor for changing his life, and now it was too late.

He couldn't imagined why he'd been summoned to Delaney's office strewn with newspapers, bluebooks, index cards, even a catcher's mitt. The professor hardly clarified things as he deposited M&M's in Charles' hand and ranted against some edict from the provost while he, Charles, tried not to stare at the nude woman in the poster on the wall. "So why in hell did I call you here, Mr. Weber?" He pushed aside some books, picked up Charles' honors thesis, and began reading in a loud voice. "'If we want to measure the grandiosity of the Enlightenment, picture the twenty-one volumes of Denis Diderot's *Encyclopédie* containing 72,000 articles on subjects from Asparagus to Zimbi. The question is: did this foolhardy enterprise sidestep the divine Creator or erase Him?'" He laid the pages in Charles's hands. "I want you to know something, Weber. You're a true writer. Don't waste your gift."

With the taste of chocolate on his lips, Charles ran to Harriet's dorm room and breathlessly told her he'd changed his mind: he wasn't going to NYU grad school; he was going to write that novel.

Eighteen months later, the novel—well, really a novella—emerged. Too short for a book, too long for a magazine. Rejected by eleven agents and fourteen editors. He took the job at Scribner's in hopes of sparing other young writers undue pain, but after a few years of sending out laboriously gentle rejection letters, he quit. Even mercy-killing is, after all, fatal. Better to resuscitate has-beens.

. . .

"So the doctor said you're fine?"

"A-okay."

Without Alice, dinnertime was difficult. He and Harriet sat amid the scrape of knife and fork, the chewing and slurping, all the noise of human machinery laid bare through long silences.

"Blood pressure? Cholesterol?"

"If you don't believe me, call him yourself."

"It's just, I don't know, you seem sad."

"'Chocolate cake is so sweet it makes me sad.' Remember? Alice said that."

Once upon a time they used to stroll along the sidewalk swinging her between them—one, two, three, whee! It turned out that she was also keeping them aloft. In the beginning Aunt Luce put him to bed, in the end he put her to bed.

They carried their dessert plates to the living room and sat side by side on the couch watching the same old news. The Republican Convention would open tonight with Reagan's valedictory. There was a heat wave in the east, a drought in the west and south, fires running rampant across Montana.

"Isn't that where she's hiking?"

"For God's sake, Chaz, you asked me that last night and I told you no, she's a hundred miles south of there."

"I forgot."

There were no phones in the Rocky Mountains. No mailboxes. He had to depend on astral messages.

They sat on the couch eating chocolate cake. The vivacious white-haired woman on TV was discussing laxatives with her husband.

"The cake's delicious, darling," Harriet said.

He nodded as the husband joined his wife in song.

"But what in the world will we do with the other fourteen pieces?" Harriet said with a little laugh.

He shrugged.

"Any momentous events at the Almanac today?"

"Well, I finally finished off Ella Wheeler Wilcox."

"Who?"

"Never mind."

A glistening, golden bottle of beer filled the screen as he felt the couch shake, saw her plate bounce on the rug, and she was standing over him. "Stop punishing me."

"Harriet!"

"I'm sick of your moping. She hasn't been murdered. She's left home. That's what daughters do: they grow up and leave."

He raised his hands, palms up. "Don't lecture me."

"She's gone, but I'm still here."

He stared at the white plate smeared with chocolate between his bare feet.

"Chaz?"

He closed his eyes. A softened voice, a few generous words, that's all that were called for, but his teeth pressed together and he thought of nothing. Nothing at all.

"Chaz!" His name had a note of desperation. "Look at me."

He shook his head.

"Look," she said in a choked voice. She was unbuttoning her blouse, slowly, until it spread open and slid off her shoulders onto the floor. She reached back, unhooked her bra, held it dangling there for a moment, and dropped it in his lap. "Skinny-dipping." Her milk-white breasts wobbled.

She was trying to smile. "Remember?"

A warm bath, with a bottle of cold white wine on the edge of the tub. Preceded by Strip Gin Rummy. Followed by sex. Games they'd played before Alice came to play with them.

She reached down for his hands. "Shall we?"

But it wasn't to be that easy. They folded themselves into the soapy water, face to face, her legs sliding under his knees, his feet propped beside her buttocks, while water slopped onto the floor. "How did we used to do this?" she said.

"We've gotten too fat for skinny-dipping."

She rubbed the washcloth down his chest. "Remember how we used to sing 'Home on the Range' in two-part harmony?"

He closed his eyes and heard the melody playing thinly in his memory, a single wavering violin, "where the deer and the antelope play," skidding off key like a child practicing alone in her room. "And the skies are not cloudy all day." Silence. Heat, sickening heat. He wanted to open his eyelids but a heavy heat had sealed them. And suddenly the vision of an ash-covered landscape swept in on him, vast and gray, as far as he could see. He raised his hands but it swept closer. He began to weep.

"Darling!" she said, taking his hands. "Poor darling."

She held him and whispered to him until the tears stopped. He opened his eyes. For a long time they looked at each other while the soapsuds broke between their legs with little crackling sounds.

"Talk to me," she said.

He shook his head. It was too awful.

"Yes," she insisted.

"I saw something. Ashes. A blanket of gray ashes stretching for miles." He took a breath. "With no one out there."

She waited for more, but there was no more. She contemplated him, working through some thought, and then she stroked his knee. "Let's go bed."

Long after she fell asleep, he lay on his back, staring into the darkness. He used to lie here at dawn while Alice sang to herself in the crib like a forest of birds. Long happy songs in the language she'd brought from the country where she'd lived before.

She was gone. He must say goodbye.

Harriet shifted her hips and sighed.

He should have written to Professor Delaney. But it wasn't too late. In the morning he'd go to the library and take out Delaney's books. Contact the University for information about his career. Interview his colleagues, his wife and children for anecdotes to flesh out the article. And who knows, maybe he'd put in his own reminiscences. That would be something new for the *Almanac*.

The Dangers of Everyday Life

Having grown up in Manhattan, that steeply vertical city, I feel overcome by the flatness of Phoenix. Even now, after eight years. On clear mornings, I sometimes climb onto the roof of my house and, with downtown at my back, look eastward over row upon row of brown-shingled roofs fenced by streets that aim straight as arrows mile after mile until they plunge into that desert toward the mountains I know are out there but, even on tiptoe, I can't see. Between the bleached sky above and parched land below, I feel desperately small and alone.

So I scramble down to make my daily round along our cul-de-sac, San Pedro Drive, which is tucked like an apostrophe among the unswerving streets. There's Juniper Bell, dressed in her baggy Phoenix Zoo uniform, watering the agave plant outside her bungalow. "Hey, Sam," she calls out in her rusty voice. "Can you believe it: forty-seven days without rain." The agave, already twice her height, is preparing any year now to do its bloom-once-and-die magic.

"That's why they call it the desert," I say.

Next comes Tristano's ocean-blue Cape. When he moved in four years ago, his house was green—a good honest green, I thought. But he painted it blue, Atlantic blue, the color he wanted to remember from Maine. He's disclosed little else about his past: a teaching job and unnamed wife in Portland; emphysema; disability insurance. "An artist living on disability, now that's a sad state of affairs, isn't it," he has said with a cackle more than a few times over the years.

He's on the porch, smoking a cigarette and drinking something that looks suspiciously like white wine. "Hello, Sam. How's our Rabbi of San Pedro this morning?"

"Same as usual," I say as usual.

"Maybe today I'll sell a painting and you'll sell a book."

"And maybe it'll rain."

Down in the cul of the cul-de-sac, at the curb by the Wigginses' cinderblock house, Tex's orange Allied "The Careful" Movers van is recuperating between hauls. "Big Daddy," he calls it. He's galloping on hands and knees across the yard with Conner on his back, while Leila sits on the front steps leafing through a magazine. "Howdy, Sam," Tex says as he pulls up beside me. I reach down to hug Conner, but all I get is the slightest touch of his arm before they're galloping away. Leila never looks up.

Heat is already rising from the asphalt, licking the soles of my feet. I trudge back toward my house at the neck of the sac of San Pedro—my house, and for Hanukah, Easter and a month in the summer, my son Billy's house. But when he's thirteen he can choose to live with me full time.

·   ·   ·

On our honeymoon, my now-ex-wife Marla and I drove almost nonstop from Chapel Hill to Phoenix with the U-haul trailer wobbling behind us, pulling our newly wedded possessions toward her job at the Maricopa Assessors' Office, my adjunct professorship at the A.S.U. School of Journalism, and our rented house.

It was supposed to have been an intimate cross-country cruise, the owl and the pussycat in a VW bus. But as the land began flattening out, I began to feel subdued and gradually we grew tired of talking over the incessant whine of the engine. We turned on the radio but when it pulled in nothing but country music we turned it off, so that by the middle of Oklahoma there was only the engine whine and the slip-slap of the pages of the home-furnishings catalogue she was reading. Between each page she licked her thumb, like a woman slowly counting money.

"What are you looking for?" I asked.

"Just looking."

"Want to play a game?"

"Like what?"

"Let's try naming the states in alphabetical order."

As we reached Hawaii, she said, "When are we going to stop?"

"As soon as you want to stop."

She stared out at the fields. "There's nothing out there."

Phoenix was intended as merely a way-station toward something better, which in her mind was a home on the California coast where she could walk on the beach and which in my mind was . . . well, I didn't know. Marriage and job were as much as I could imagine.

By the fourth day, we were in the Painted Desert. All afternoon she napped while I drove across a landscape that stretched flatter and farther than I had ever seen. Even through dark green glasses, even at five o'clock, the sun made me squint. I needed to pee, so I pulled off the highway, turned off the motor, and stepped outside.

A vast heat bore down upon me. It swept across the land and down from the sky, blanketing my face, shoving my breath down my throat. I raised a hand to defend myself. I could die in this desert before anyone saved me. One snap of the fan belt, one mistake, and after a few hours beneath this merciless sun. . . .

"For God's sake, Sam. What are you doing out there?"

I was about to zip up my pants when I recalled the picture in my *Children's Bible Stories*: the robed, bearded Jews dancing in their desert around a golden calf. They were dancing too gleefully to notice the figure who loomed behind them in the upper right corner. Moses, in dark purple robe with glittering eyes. Moses, who had just returned from talking with Yahweh on the mount. "Children of Israel!" Moses roared. "Is that how you behave when I'm gone!" Smashing the two tablets inscribed with the words of God, he ordered every man to slay his brother, every man his companion, every man his neighbor.

I pulled open the door and jumped in. Turned on the motor. Flicked the fan to high. Sped down the highway with the U-haul wobbling madly behind us.

"What's wrong?" Marla asked.

"Maybe we shouldn't have done this."

"A little late for that."

Forty years wandering in the desert before they would reach their homeland. The rest of a man's life.

· · ·

When I wasn't rehired by the J School, I fell back onto what I knew best, namely books and Brooklyn. "'Flatbush of the Desert'—Sam Jacobson, Rare and Historic Books about Brooklyn—bought and sold—catalogues issued." That's how my ad reads in *The AB Bookman's Yearbook*. Who would have believed there are so many books about Brooklyn? To a Manhattan boy, that borough seemed merely the city's afterthought, where the Dodgers used to play and the Coney Island Steeplechase had burned down: the end of the subway line. But here I am with two thousand books on Hasidic Jews, the Navy Yard, the Bridge, Walt Whitman at the *Eagle*, Jackie Robinson and the boys of summer—two thousand books plus who knows how many more every time I come back from another auction or estate sale. They fill half the attic, rise shoulder-high on all four living-room walls, heap along the hall so you have to walk sideways, and the newcomers rest in cardboard boxes out there in the carport.

. . .

The day the Wigginses moved in, we chatted in the cool shadow of the van. Tex was wearing a Padres baseball cap, jeans, no shirt, and his arms were so thickly muscled that mine felt like tinker toys. She stood half-hidden behind him, hands clasped over her ballooning belly. "I'm Tex," he said, "and this pretty little lady's my wife Leila. And any day now, you'll be seeing our baby."

It turned out Tex was from Kentucky and Leila from West Virginia and they had always dreamed of living where you see nothing but sky for fifty miles in every direction.

"More like fifty yards during rush-hour smog," I said.

He pointed toward my garage, where stacks of cardboard boxes rose higher than the roof of my VW bus. "Looks like you just arrived yourself."

"Five years ago, actually. Those are my books."

"That's a whole lot of backed-up reading."

"I'm a book dealer. I buy and sell."

"You mean you don't read the insides."

That's right, Tex, I thought. Used and rare books pass unread through my hands the way people's love-blotched mattresses pass through yours. But your mattresses find their way to new homes, whereas my books wait for months, years, inside those boxes in my garage. These thoughts seemed a bit much for a first conversation, however, so I stepped sideways to see his wife. "I hope you'll like it out here. Arizona takes getting used to."

"Maybe so," she said.

"She's kinda shy to start with," Tex said, "but don't let that fool you, Sam." He winked.

It seemed like one of those man-to-man boasts about last night's woman, but she was his wife and she was right here listening. I shrugged an apology toward Leila, but her face was impassive. She had a thin-lipped mouth, brown hair pulled back by a rubber band—no hint of that lusty excitement Tex had winked about.

"Like he said," she murmured, "don't let it fool you."

Before I could decipher that, she turned and punched his shoulder hard enough to leave a little dent from her ring.

· · ·

On the night of Marla's thirty-first birthday, Billy was asleep in his crib. Marla and I were in the kitchen, cleaning the dinner plates and waging yet another of our arguments. This one was about the bracelet I'd bought her.

"How much did it cost?" she asked.

"My mother would say that's a rude question."

"Your usual extravagance?"

"I'd prefer 'generosity.'" I thumbed chocolate icing from the cake. "Better yet, a simple 'thank you.'"

"Fine, thanks, but that doesn't pay next month's Visa bill."

"Must you turn everything into money?"

"Let's be glad someone around here does."

"Don't start that again, Marla. You agreed to give the book business two more years before deciding whether—"

"In two years I'll be middle-aged."

Trying to keep our voices down so as not to wake Billy. Standing too close because of him. Her face was swollen. Blotchy.

"Thirty-one years old," she said, "and what kind of life do we have? I don't want to wait forever to live in a decent house."

"Well, don't wait."

"And just what does that mean?"

"Whatever the fuck you want it to mean," I said, waving a fist.

"Go on, hit me. Get it over with."

There was a squishy sound as I slammed my fist into the cake. Her blouse and hair were speckled with icing. One thought and a second thought went across her face. She took slow steps backwards, keeping her eyes on me until she reached the doorway and turned, walked down the hall, closed the bedroom door with a click. Billy moaned once in his crib. I pressed a hand against my mouth, tasted semi-sweet chocolate, and bit down on my knuckle until a few tears came. Only a few.

I spent the night on the living-room couch. In the morning, I saw the open suitcase on our bed. She stood beside the bureau, fully dressed.

"It won't happen again," I said.

She swept the back of her hand through the air. On ordinary mornings that would have meant "no problem," but this morning her hand was sweeping me out of her way.

"We'll go back to that marriage counselor," I said.

She shook her head.

"Marla. Please!"

"Not this time." She was folding underpants in a corner of the suitcase, glossy pink and white and red layers, unbearably pretty.

"Where are you going?"

"Rob and Fran's."

"Makes sense." Yes, I welcomed the idea of a day or two alone with my books and Billy. "When you come back, we'll figure things out."

She bent over the bureau drawer.

"How long do you think you'll be gone?" I asked.

She straightened up, holding a handful of bras against her chest, and looked at me. Just looked at me. Finally she turned and laid the bras in the suitcase. So much underwear. Enough to last a month. A lifetime.

I felt dizzy. Braced an elbow on the bureau. This was it. After all those fights and truces. "Get out, then." I felt a rush of gladness. "Billy and I can take care of ourselves."

"No, Sam. He goes with me."

"What?"

"I'm taking him with me."

"You. . . ." I couldn't breathe. "You can't take my son."

"Our son."

"No!" My flesh and blood. "It would kill me."

"This is hard enough. Don't try and make me feel guilty." Her face was a mask.

Two rooms away, Billy was sleeping in his teddy-bear p.j.'s. I wanted to strangle her. Slowly I backed out of the room.

Twelve months later, she was back in Chapel Hill with a job, a boy friend and, of course, our son. Divorced beyond recall.

Hanukah, Easter and a month in the summer.

. . .

A year or so ago, I came upon Tex sitting in his yard with a glistening bottle of beer in one hand while, with the other, he rolled a ball back and forth with Conner. "Pull up a chair, Sam. How about a beer?"

"Thanks, but I never drink before noon." I helped Conner climb up the yellow slide and caught him at the bottom. Again. And again.

"Sold many books lately?" Tex asked.

"Yesterday someone in Atlanta bought a first-edition *Coney Island of the Mind*. That'll pay this month's rent." Little boy legs are pudgy and smooth, with knees like pink marshmallows, needing protection against scrapes and falls. "When's your next trip?"

"Tomorrow I haul ass up to Portland and Spokane." He took Conner onto his lap. "One of these days, buddy, I'm gonna take you with me. Away from your miserable mama."

I felt a twinge of jealousy, watching him wrap his arms around his son. "I bet you and Leila could use a break. If you want to go see a movie, I'd be glad to babysit."

"Thanks, but a movie ain't going to cure whatever's eating at her." He pulled up his left sleeve and traced a puffy red wound along the shoulder. "Here's what she did the day before yesterday."

"Oh my god."

"With a grapefruit knife." Tex stood up, cradling Conner in one arm. "If you want, come play with the boy while I'm up in Portland."

The next afternoon I knocked at their door and heard a fraught conversation inside. "She's been like this ever since Todd went into his coma." "I'm going to phone Dr. Wilson and tell him to come over right away." A soap opera. I knocked harder.

When Leila opened the door, her eyes had a glazed quality. "Oh, it's you."

"I thought I'd see how you and Conner are getting along

while Tex is gone."

"Come on in." We stepped over shoes and toys and a plate of scrambled eggs as she led me through the kitchen into the TV room. "Excuse the mess, but I've got to take care of everything single-handed around here. Plus the baby was up half the night crying. He finally fell asleep an hour ago."

"I'm sure it's hard without Tex."

We had to raise our voices over the soap opera. "Oh, a lot of help he is." With one foot she nudged a toy fire engine under the couch. "I'm sick to death of this godforsaken place. If my vote counted for anything, we'd be back with my folks in West Virginia."

Go, I wanted to scream, *and leave your son with someone who loves him.* But what I said was, "Anything I can do for you?"

She shrugged and turned to watch the TV. I stood there, wondering how to prolong the conversation until Conner awoke. On the TV screen, a young blond woman was dancing across a bright green meadow with a tube of antiperspirant in her hand. Finally I walked out.

· · ·

Whenever I opened my cutlery drawer, I thought of that grapefruit knife. But Tex never mentioned it again and life on San Pedro continued as usual. Until this morning.

I'm in my pajamas, barefoot, poaching an egg when Tex's van rumbles slowly past the kitchen window. He's grim-faced, with Conner beside him. I run outside and shout, "Is everything okay?" Conner waves and laughs as if it were one of our games. Tex pretends not to hear, guns the motor, swings wide right, and speeds west toward who knows where.

What happened this time? A peaceful goodbye or a bloody fight? As I look toward their house, my feet begin to burn on the asphalt. I can't go down there now, and why should I care anyhow? Back in my kitchen, I spoon the egg out of the boiling water into a bowl. It lies there, slick and seamless. Then it gives a little shudder and yolk gushes out. I love poached eggs but my throat is clogged with anxiety.

I dial Leila's number; let it ring six times, seven, eight. If she's gone somewhere, wouldn't I have seen her car passing? I get dressed and am putting on my shoes to walk down there when the phone rings.

"Yes?" I said softly, ready for whatever she might tell me.

"Hi, Dad." It's Billy—his Saturday-morning call—his voice piping from North Carolina across all those mountains and flatlands, sounding so vivid that when I close my eyes I can imagine him standing here, six years old, in T-shirt and jeans, barefoot, or maybe in unmatched socks, within arms' reach. "Guess what Mom and Jim are giving me for my birthday. They're taking me to the Tar Heels—Duke game." A month till Easter—four months since I've buckled him into the airplane seat and kissed his forehead—another five months of my son's life I'll never know. "And guess what. Jim says after the game we'll try 'n get Dean Smith's autograph."

By the time we're done comparing the Heels to the Sun Devils and he's told me about biking down a big hill too fast and going over the handle bars but his elbow doesn't hurt too bad now—by the time he says "I love you, too, Dad" and I open my eyes, I've forgotten why I'm wearing only one shoe. I sit with the phone in my lap, just sit here, while the sadness sloshes inside me.

Finally I force myself to get up, make the bed, make lasagna, vacuum the living room—the familiar ploys to siphon off the sadness. And to postpone finding out what Tex and Leila have done to each other.

I turn off the vacuum cleaner and dial her number. Still no answer.

I go outside, look down the street and see nothing out of the ordinary: asphalt and palm trees rippling behind heat waves. Is Leila pacing from room to room, still seething with the rage that caused him to take Conner and leave? Or is she sobbing on the bed, abandoned by an uncaring husband?

And meanwhile Tex and Conner are eating Oreos and singing "Row, row your boat," or whatever sweet rituals they share. Lucky Tex. What's the difference, I wonder, between a loving father and a kidnapper?

If Tex hasn't come home by dinnertime, or if Leila hasn't answered the phone, I promise I'll walk down there.

·   ·   ·

An hour ago Leila still didn't answer the phone. After that

I was negotiating with a woman in Seattle who finally decided to buy a first edition of Alfred Kazin's *New York Jew* (dust jacket very good, slight foxing on the fore edge, back cover has minor edgewear and sunning, $42). The third sale this week. To celebrate, I've eaten an early dinner so I can catch the seven o'clock show of Woody Allen's new film. My tongue is seeking bits of lasagna between my teeth as I walk down the street. By now, Tex and Conner will be hundreds of miles away, in Nevada or maybe California, speeding relentlessly away inside "Big Daddy."

"Hey, Sam," Juniper Bell calls out. "Can you believe it's been sixty-two days without rain?"

"Have you seen Leila today?"

She shrugs. "I haven't noticed."

I pass Tristano's yard and hear his husky cough. "Hello there, rabbi." He steps out from behind the prickly pear, which is where he hides cigarettes from himself, and exhales a puff of smoke.

"Have you seen Leila?"

"Haven't seen her and haven't looked." He strokes his white beard, which is flecked purple and green. "Come in for a cold beer and prevent me from ruining this damn canvas any further."

"Not now. I'm going to the new Woody Allen movie. Do you want to join me?"

"Thanks, but movies make my eyes tear up."

"Leila hasn't answered her phone all day."

"Maybe a friend came by and they went to see the Grand Canyon."

"She doesn't have any friends."

He squeezes my shoulder. "Forget about her and have fun with Woody."

I take a few steps down the street and peer between the palm trees. The Wigginses' lawn mower stands in the tall brown grass. The front door is closed. The garage door is closed. Toys in the yard, laundry on the line. Except for the twisted string of Christmas lights blinking on the saguaro cactus, everything seems ordinary and subdued.

I hate being late for a movie. I'll go down to Leila tomorrow.

. . .

A man's supposed to take care of the garbage, flat tires, the burglar downstairs. The dangers of everyday life. But whose job is it when Tex and Conner have sped past your door toward God-knows-where and this morning, twenty-four hours later, Leila still doesn't answer the phone?

San Pedro lies quiet, this Sunday morning. The black curtain is pulled tight across Juniper Bell's window. The sun is shoulder-high, orange turning white, but the air still holds on to some of last night's coolness. Silence drifts moodily along our cul-de-sac.

Tristano is on his porch doing finger exercises. "How was Woody Allen?"

"Terrible. It was one of his attempts at being tragic."

"He should resign himself to being funny." And then he says something else, which I don't hear because I'm walking down the street.

I ring their doorbell, twice, three and four times. Yesterday's mail is in the box. I feel the skin tighten at the corners of my eyes. With small steps I begin to circle the house, window after window. The living room is neat and unoccupied. Their bedroom is unoccupied, blankets smooth, closet doors shut. I turn the corner. The bathroom, at least the wedge I can see under the shade, is unoccupied. Conner's room is disturbed: a jumble of clothes on the floor, a chair tipped backward, a teddy bear on its stomach on the table beside three cigarette butts. I picture Billy's room in my house where the new seven-speed bicycle waits to surprise him.

As I turn the next corner, I hear a man's voice coming from the garage. ". . . and a high today of ninety-two, down to the mid-seventies tonight." I walk faster along the side of the garage and find a window. The glass is cold against my forehead. At first I can see only the chrome bumper of the car. Then I see a little radio on the hood and, off to the left, hanging from the wall, the gleam of shears and a wide-tooth saw. ". . . no hope of rain in greater Phoenix this week. . . ." I squint into a shadowed corner until I make out a yellow stool tipped over. And then the oblong shape stretched between ceiling and floor. Bare feet, arms, the back of her head cocked at a curious angle. Unmoving. In midair. And although I can't see the rope. . . . And although I can't see the rope. . . .

"Help!" I'm stumbling up the street, blinded by light, screaming, "help! Oh my God!"

Soon, ambulances and police cars convene at the end of the cul-de-sac, their blue and red lights flashing against the sunshine. Metallic voices speak from the empty front seats: "Two Indian males running out of Paradise Valley Mall. Do you read?" "Roger. Ten four."

A policeman stands in front of the garage, thumbs hooked over his belt, blank-faced. Men in white uniforms are busy inside.

Juniper Bell wears a wide straw hat and is eating an orange. Every now and then she says to no one in particular: "It's what you get."

Tristano leans against an ambulance, smoking, coughing.

"If only I'd come down here yesterday," I murmur.

"No, rabbi," he says. "You're not responsible."

"She didn't answer the phone. I should have realized. If I'd just walked down here, maybe—"

"Nonsense, Sam." A burst of static spurts from the police car. "We can barely save ourselves."

But Conner is safe. Tex made sure of that. He and his son were thirty miles south of Sacramento when the Allied Van dispatcher radioed them. They can't be back before nightfall, even driving at top speed. How in god's name will Tex explain to Conner that he doesn't have a mommy?

I stare at the garage and taste the anger at the back of my

mouth. So what if she was miserable! No mother who's any kind of loving mother should have done this.

Two men come out of the garage bearing a stretcher that holds a long, untidy gray sack. "Okay, folks, it's all over," the policeman says. "Go on home."

As I walk up the street, a peculiar emotion fills me, buoyant, large. I want Billy. I'm filled with want. With the pain of desire to feel his cheek against mine and fold his hand inside mine and hear him breathe at night in the next room.

I stop, squint toward the sun climbing the bone-white sky. The roofs, the clouds, everything is sharply outlined. Burningly clear. I don't belong here. I belong with my son.

I jog to catch up with Tristano. "I'm leaving."

He waves the cigarette. "See you tomorrow."

"No, I'm leaving for good. Back to North Carolina. To my son."

"Going home." He takes a puff, coughs, shakes his head. "Lucky you." His thin smile is overwhelmed by the sadness in his eyes.

"Come east and visit me."

"Sure, right after my solo show opens at the Guggenheim." He spreads his arms and we join in a smoky embrace. "Stop in for a cold beer before you go, rabbi."

SUBJECT TO OUTBREAKS OF RECKLESS LOVE

When she went outside in her bathrobe to pick up the newspaper, the boy was sitting on the top step of her porch, like a package that had been delivered overnight, knees pulled up to his chin. Except she hadn't ordered a package.

"Hello, I'm Ellen, and who might you be?" she said in the soft, unhurried voice with which she greeted new clients at the clinic.

"I'm Billy. I'm six-and-a-half but the doctor said I'm as tall as seven." He wore clean blue pants and a matching shirt, maybe even ironed, so he wasn't your typical abandoned or runaway child, but what was he?

"Are you lost?"

"No, I live down there," pointing down Curtis Road.

"But now you're sitting here?"

"Unh huh."

"Shouldn't you be in school, Billy?"

"It's a teacher work day."

He gazed at her patiently, unperturbed, his eyes brimming with good nature. She cinched her robe tighter. As an experienced social worker, of course she knew what she ought to do, which was to resist succumbing to sentimentality? On the other hand, it would be more efficient to avoid the brouhaha of those Social Service bureaucrats by taking him home herself. And he was, undeniably, cute as hell. "It's cold out here, Billy. Do you want to come inside and have some hot chocolate?"

"Yes, please," he said, scrambling to his feet, scooping up the newspaper, bouncing ahead of her into the house.

"Turn left," she called, but he had already turned left, and by the time she'd closed the door and hustled down the hallway he was sitting cross-legged on a kitchen chair—Vince's chair—as if he lived here. A mix of delight and grief, both at once, buffeted her. She steadied herself with one hand against the table. "I need to phone your parents. They're going to wonder where you are."

"Don't worry. My mom went to her office and said for me to watch TV until Jim shows up, but all he ever does is type on his computer instead of playing with me, so I decided to go exploring."

"Who's Jim?"

"My mom's boy friend. Do you have any marshmallows?"

"I'm afraid not."

"That's okay. What are those for?" He pointed at the five yellow bowls lined up on the floor.

"Cats." She poured milk and cocoa into a saucepan. "How do you feel about cats?"

"They're good, I guess, but not as good as dogs, and penguins are my favorite. What's your favorite animal?"

"I don't know." She stirred figure-eights in the cocoa. Vince used to rehearse his class lecture between or even during mouthfuls of scrambled eggs and bacon, demanding her critiques as if she were a devotée of French history, but after a year and a half of silence she felt out of practice for breakfast conversation, especially about animals. Still, Billy was looking expectantly at her. "I like giraffes," she said.

"Giraffes eat sixty pounds of leaves a day, which sounds really disgusting." He stuck out his tongue. "And boring. Where are the cats?"

"They're hiding because they're shy." And petrified to have a child in their domain. She poured the steaming cocoa into the purple mug, "*saiser le jour.*" Which had sat all these months on the cupboard as if waiting for this opportunity.

"I'm not shy."

"I noticed." This was getting out of hand. When a child arrived at the clinic, she was the one who asked the questions on the three-page intake form. But here *she* was being taken in by this blithely inquisitive visitor who seemed to have no notion of leaving.

He blew lustily into the mug. "I bet you didn't know that giraffes sleep only half an hour every day. Standing up."

"Really. How do you know all this?"

"From a library book. I learned to read in September." He opened the newspaper and, in step with his index finger, recited, "Tar Heels Win in Last-Minute Surge."

It was unsettling but also—how should she put it?—bracing to hold a discussion about giraffes before her first cup of coffee. And yes, even if they were lacking in what Vince would call "intellectual rigor," she had to admit she preferred giraffes to the rise and fall of Robespierre. She took her coffee and English muffin to the table and watched Billy puffing and sipping. His hair was a whirligig of light brown curls spilling down to delicate eyebrows that arched over green—almost turquoise—eyes.

"So tell me, Billy: why did you come to my house?"

As he smiled, a dimple formed beside his damp brown mustache. "Because you have hot chocolate." She laughed, and he wriggled in the chair, pleased with himself. "Can I look for the cats?"

"Go ahead."

She had just finished her muffin when she heard him calling: "This is so cool."

She found him in Vince's study, where he was revolving on the desk chair, the catcher's mitt in one hand, the snow globe of Notre Dame Cathedral in the other. "I bet I could catch a fast ball with this mitt and my hand wouldn't even sting." He stopped revolving and pointed the mitt toward the yellowing photograph of the St. Ignatius baseball team on the wall. "Which one is he?"

"Who?"

"The boy who owns this glove. Your son."

"He's in the middle on the front row." Chubby-cheeked, the familiar crooked smile: a junior, beardless Vince. "But he's my husband, not my son. That photo comes from a long time ago. "

"Where is he?" he said, looking around, as if Vince were upstairs getting dressed, or hiding like the cats.

She fought down the old pain in her chest. "He's gone."

"To his office?"

She shouldn't have let him in, this charmer with all his knife-sharp questions. "No, he's gone and he's never coming back." He stiffened, a stricken look on his face, as if she had slapped him. "But I'm getting used to it."

He shook the snow globe and they watched the white flakes swim onto Notre Dame. "My dad's gone in Arizona," Billy said. "But he promised to come back and see me at Easter."

"Lucky you." She reached down and stroked his head— such lush curls. "Play with Vince's things while I get dressed."

Later, walking down Curtis Road, they were silent, as if they were old friends who would be parting. It felt odd to have someone walking beside her, especially—after being childless all these years—a small someone. She wanted to take his hand, but she didn't feel she had the right.

"Here's my house," he said. Uneven black letters on the mailbox announced "Jacobson". At the front door she spread her arms and he pressed his forehead against her chest. His shoulder blades were like little wings under her hands. Pleasure shuddered through her, beating in her throat, so much pleasure that it was painful and she released him.

"I had fun," he murmured.

"Me too."

As Billy pushed the door and dashed in, a youngish man—unshaven, wearing a baseball cap and red flannel shirt—looked up from typing on a computer. "Billy? What the hell? All this time I thought you were up in your room."

"I was playing outside."

"And I brought him home," she said. She and Billy exchanged a look, conspirators in not quite a lie.

As she drove to the clinic, an NPR newscaster was describing the damage from Saddam Hussein's Scud missiles that hit Israel yesterday. She turned off the radio. When was the last time she'd had fun? During the first months of widowhood, while rage and despair and self-pity sluiced though her, the closest approximation of fun she could muster was to sprawl on the couch at night and listen to Bach's cello concertos until, with the help of a glass of wine, sometimes two glasses, she was soothed or at least fatigued enough to sleep. Fun required someone to have it with, like ballroom dancing or Scrabble. Fun is a transitive noun. She smiled. *A transitive noun?* Vince would say with his high-pitched laugh, tracing a check mark on the air. *Score one, Sweetpea.*

The traffic thickened as she neared Durham, a relentless metallic herd speeding sixty-five miles per hour, drivers hunched grimly in the saddles. Suppose she took this exit and drove back to Chapel Hill, to Redbud Lane, and. . . . And what? *Hello, Jim, I realize you've known me for all of two minutes, but I'd like to take Billy to the playground.* Ridiculous. A neighbor might borrow a cup of sugar, but not a child.

Her knuckles hurt, gripping the steering wheel as she passed the exit.

.   .   .

Dear Mrs. Delaney. Please forgive this intrusion. I'm a former student of Professor Delaney's from the late Sixties.

The letter was lurking in the pile of bills that afternoon. Crisp stationery, with a blue letterhead announcing *The Almanac of Has-Beens.*

He had an inspiring influence on me and countless others not only in the classroom but beyond. Now, twenty-some years later, I would like to return the favor by writing about him in the next edition of The Almanac of Has-Beens. *Would you be willing to talk with me on the phone?*

No, Mr. Charles Weber, she did not forgive the intrusion. Harassing enough those tedious discussions with the lawyer, the accountant and the University Human Resources officer, who had handled the legal and economic remains of "your late husband" or "your departed husband." Vince would have had a field day. "Make up your minds, gentlemen," he would have said. "Am I late or departed? Coming or going?" Or worse, he would have lurched into his Groucho Marx imitation, singing "I'm glad I came, but just the same, I must be going," wagging an invisible cigar, embarrassing everyone but himself.

Dear Mr. Weber, she wrote below his signature. *Much as I appreciate your admiration for Professor Delaney, I regret that I am too occupied at this time to consider an interview for your Almanac. Sincerely....*

It sounded a bit queenly, but at least it would close the door on Mr. Weber.

The next day when she arrived home from work, Billy was standing on the porch, grinning and waving. She fumbled to open the car door, clumsy with happiness. "What are you doing here?"

"After-school ended early, so I came here until Mom gets home at 5:00."

Forty-five minutes. Not a precious minute to waste, then. "Come on in and have a snack."

"Do you have marshmallows?"

"Not this time. But how about a chocolate chip cookie?"

"My favorite. I used to like Oreos when I was young, but one day I had too many and threw up."

Not this time? As if there would be a next time. Why was she indulging this sense of hope? Dangerous giddy hope.

They had cookies and lemonade, after which they knelt on the floor of Vince's study and stationed his Napoleonic toy soldiers around the cardboard model of Versailles. Koshka and Minou emerged, sniffed Billy from head to toe, and rubbed against his legs. "Hello, kitty cats," he said. "I'm General Bill."

Shortly after the soldiers marched off to Russia under the desk, he pointed toward the bookshelves. "My dad has a hundred times more books than that."

"Is he a professor?"

"No, he sells books." He stroked Koshka, who was purring at his feet. "Do you think the other cats will come out next time?"

"I hope so."

It was five minutes past five when they parked outside his house and his mother was in the doorway, screaming. "Billy! Where have you been?"

"At Ellen's house. We had chocolate chip cookies and played with the toy soldiers. Don't be mad, Mom."

"I've been worried sick." She hugged him. "Go to your room. I need to talk to this woman." She turned, short dark hair framing dark, furious eyes. "What do you think you're doing with my son?" Beneath her black pants-suit her body was rigid.

"I'm Ellen Delaney from Curtis Drive." She stretched out a hand, but Mrs. Jacobson waved it away. "Billy showed up on my doorstep yesterday and again today, I've no idea why."

"And you took him in and fed him cookies? A strange

woman feeding somebody else's child?"

The witch who almost ate Hansel and Gretel. How could she have been so stupid? "I'm sorry I scared you, but he's so delightful, and when he showed up I thought the best thing was to take him in, but I should have phoned." The words were tumbling out helterskelter, ruining everything. "I meant no harm." She looked past Mrs. Jacobson up the shadowy stairs toward Billy, somewhere up there in his room, beyond reach. "Billy's a lovely boy." She backed away. Oh god, she pushed back the tears with both hands. "Forgive me."

"Okay, okay." Mrs. Jacobson's face and shoulders softened. "I shouldn't have jumped on you, but I was scared out of my mind."

"Of course. Who wouldn't be."

"My goddamn boy friend's the one I need to yell at. He was supposed to be here."

"I'm sorry."

"If only I could hire a nanny, but I'm a single mother with a fulltime job with crappy pay."

You can hire me, she thought, but when Mrs. Jacobson startled and said "You?" she realized she'd said it aloud.

"Yes, me. I'm dependable and I'd love to take care of him."

"No." She surveyed Ellen head to foot. "No, I don't know a thing about you. Anyhow, I couldn't afford it."

"And I'm a social worker. I'll do it for free. Please." She made fists of hope inside her pockets, watching Billy's mother probe the idea, the crazy idea, until Mrs. Jacobson laughed and said, "I can't believe this."

"Neither can I." Now they were both laughing, and she let herself believe it was going to happen.

After a half-hour of ironing out details—self-introductions; phone numbers; front-door key; her business card and a list of three references who could vouch she was, in fact, a sober, dependable social worker (though obviously susceptible to outbreaks of reckless love) —at the end of half an hour she and Marla reached agreement. Mondays, Wednesdays and Fridays at 3:15, Ellen would leave the clinic early and take Billy from school to her house.

"Billy?" his mother called out, but he was already sprinting down the stairs, shouting "hooray."

. . .

Dear Mrs. Delaney. I would be grateful if you read the enclosed essay-in-progress and make whatever suggestions and corrections you find appropriate.

The Almanac Man was back again, like a pesky suitor undaunted by her snub. She weighed the manila envelope in one hand. Well, maybe she owed him—and Vince—at least a glance.

It's 587 miles from Worcester, MA, to Chapel Hill, NC, but the cultural distance from gritty working-class neighborhood to bucolic intellectual campus is immeasurably longer and steeper. Vincent J. Delaney (1935 -1987) made that journey with remarkable agility, from St. Ignatius High School and Boston

College to Princeton University (Ph.D., 1964) to a professorship of French history at the University of North Carolina. A swift climb, but he didn't let it go to his head. He never forgot he was one of "the regular people," as he liked to call them, whether 18th-century peasants or 20th-century students. Certain lectures acquired a kind of fame in the undergraduate grapevine: the one about Dreyfus, for example, when Delaney recited by heart portions of Zola's "J'Accuse" and added analogies to President Nixon.

She barely recognized Vince—at least the Vince she knew—in this amalgam of Horatio Alger, Mr. Chips and the Reverend Martin Luther King. Too much nobility and too little bluster.

Delaney cultivated an aura of frowns and growls. But students who went to his office asking for help or, better yet, challenging something he'd said in class, found (amid the maelstrom of things on the floor and walls) a friendly reception.

And where was the wicked sense of humor? It was like looking at one of those paintings of retired dignitaries whose faces have been reupholstered into barely recognizable approximations of their middle-aged selves.

During his tragically shortened career, Professor Delaney published one book, <u>Censorship and Diderot's Encyclopédie</u>, and two articles on Rousseau. "For the last ten or fifteen years," a colleague said, "he was allegedly writing a 'blockbuster' biography of Rousseau that would turn scholars on their heads. Now we'll never know."

She knew all too well. There was no biography—only those pages that he read aloud to her after dinner and, despite her praise, he later shredded, overcome by what he called perfectionism and she, privately, called a sense of inadequacy.

Charles Weber wanted suggestions and corrections of her husband. Thank you, but for twenty-five years she had attempted all too many, in vain.

There was more, four or five single-spaced pages more, but she folded them into the envelope unread.

. . .

Monday, Wednesday, and Friday afternoons. Now that she was leaving work an hour early, some of her coworkers teased her that she was sneaking off to a tryst with a man, probably a married man, which she didn't deny, in fact she fed the flame with coy smiles, relishing the notoriety.

Sundays, Tuesdays, and Thursdays, she made sure to restock chocolate chip cookies, peanut butter and milk. And crayons with a stack of colored paper in case Billy decided to crouch on the floor to draw. And a few animal books from the public library, which he read aloud, sitting in her lap, the vibrations of his voice thrumming against her ribs as if she were accompanying him. Also the cloth mouse on a string to race the cats down the hall.

But no TV. "I'm sick of reading and drawing," he whined one afternoon, folding himself into a sulky ball on the floor. "Jim lets me watch cartoons."

"Well, I'm not Jim. If you're watching TV, we're not being really together."

"You're mean." He flailed his arms, sending the cats scurrying.

"You're scaring the cats."

"I don't care. Leave me alone."

Ten minutes later he appeared in the kitchen, where she'd been leafing blindly through a *New Yorker* and resisting the urge to appease him. He touched her arm. "Do you want to play hide and seek?"

Every Monday, Wednesday, and Friday they were together and then she was alone again in the silence of her house, but now a different silence, plump with love.

She sponged crumbs off the table, put the crayons into the drawer, taped the laughing blue dragon on the refrigerator door. On her way upstairs, she paused outside Vince's study. As soon as the moving men carried the oversized desk and chair into the attic, she could install the futon (with blankets embroidered with Tar Heel-blue basketballs) and chest of drawers she'd ordered. She felt a little anxious, not having had a sleepover in forty-five years. But Marla said don't worry, and Billy was already requesting maple syrup for his waffles at breakfast.

. . .

"Thank you for talking with me, Mrs. Delaney." In person, Charles Weber resembled not at all the lean, slick, fast-talking New Yorker she had pictured between the lines of his letters. Balding, chubby, wearing a rumpled sweater and apologetic smile, he lowered his body slowly into the armchair. "Ordinarily I'm not a pushy person, but your husband was important in my life. So while I was down here for my twenty-fifth class reunion, I couldn't resist phoning. Just in case."

His voice sank toward the end of sentences, reminding her of someone or other.

"I'm glad to help, at least for an hour," she said. "Then a friend will arrive." Namely, Billy, who was coming for lunch and a preview of the Tar Heel blankets.

"Professor Delaney gave me the courage to go to New York and write my novel. I meant to send him a thank-you letter, but I wanted to wait until the novel was published, which of course never happened." He ducked his head and mumbled something.

"What?"

"And now it's too late." He toyed with his shoelace. "But at least I can write about him in the *Almanac*."

"Who else have you written about?" Eeyore, that's whom he sounded like, the mournful donkey.

"People who once were famous, like Eugen Sandow, the strongest man in the world. But also so-called 'regular people' who deserve to be remembered." He sighed. "Regular people. Professor Delaney loved saying that."

"Yes," she said, although she didn't remember anything

of the kind.

"I'm hoping you can provide some personal details. Childhood anecdotes, hobbies, maybe a family snapshot."

She peered past the droopy cheeks and eyelids for the twenty-year-old Charles who had perched on the edge of his chair in Vince's office, craving and dreading his professor's verdict. That boy probably had an indifferent father or a dead one—yes, she'd bet a hundred dollars on it. Why deprive him of what he yearned for, even if it was a semi-fictional Vince Delaney. "I have just what you're looking for. Follow me into his study."

"Wonderful." He almost leaped out of the chair.

Let him rummage among the relics and she'd be spared his nosy questions.

"I remember that." He pointed to the catcher's mitt. "And this Mickey Mouse clock: he set it to ring two minutes before the end of class." He pulled a pad from his pocket. "Would you mind if I take some notes?"

"Have a seat. And look at these files of his lectures, if you want."

She busied herself in the kitchen, making ham-and-cheese sandwiches, pouring lemonade, laying out the twisty plastic straw. "Everything okay?" she called out to Weber.

"Marvelous. I feel twenty-five years younger." Half-past noon. Billy was twenty minutes late. She dialed his number.

"Hello?" Billy's voice chirped like a bird.

"Hi. It's Ellen. I thought you were coming for lunch."

"Ellen? Oh, I forgot. You see, my dad just phoned and you'll never guess what he said, it's the best news ever. Come over here and I'll tell you all about it. Bye"

She put down the phone and stared at it. What kind of news would make him forget? Well, whatever it was, at least he wanted to share it with her.

"I'm sorry, Mr. Weber, but I'm afraid I have to go out and meet someone briefly."

He was sitting in Vince's chair, hunched over pages strewn across the desk. "Already?" He looked up at her. "I'd hoped. . . . You know. . . ." He gestured toward the desk.

Poor Eeyore. She had made him a promise, but Billy was waiting to share his tantalizing news. "I can't believe I'm saying this, but what if you stayed here while I go off for fifteen or twenty minutes."

"I'll guard everything with my life."

Before she risked second-guessing her foolishness, she grabbed the car keys and drove faster than the speed limit down Curtis Road.

"Guess what." Billy was bouncing on the porch when she arrived. "You'll never guess in a hundred years." He stretched both arms above his head. "My dad's moving here from Arizona. For keeps! He's going to rent a house near us and maybe have a dog and I'll go there on weekends for sleepovers. Isn't that terrific?"

"Oh yes. Terrific." She pictured the blue basketball

blankets in her closet. "I'm so happy for you." She gave him a kiss. "When will he come?"

"Soon. Maybe next month, so we can go to July Fourth fireworks."

She sustained her smile while he chattered on, until after another kiss she retreated to her car and drove away. So that was his big news. Sleepovers at Dad's house. She was glad for him, of course she was, but she couldn't help feeling disappointed. No, resentful. She pounded the steering wheel. After all the cookies and library books and basketball blankets—suddenly none of it counted.

A car horn beeped angrily. Oops, she'd gone straight through that stop sign.

Billy would be surrounded now by his mother and her boy friend Jim and his father, while she stood on the outside, struggling to reach over their shoulders, the woman on Curtis Road.

She drove slowly up the long hill until she couldn't see through the tears and pulled sideways onto the grass. Turned off the engine. Laid her forehead against the steering wheel.

"Hello?" Someone was knocking against the window. "Are you all right?"

She lifted her head and nodded, but he didn't move, astride a bicycle, gazing down at her with a worried expression, leaving her no alternative but to hastily rub away the tears and lower the window. "Yes, I'm okay, thank you."

"Car trouble?"

"No, I was a little upset, that's all."

"I was bicycling by and—." His eyebrows jumped. "You're Ellen Delaney, aren't you? I'm Al Cox."

"I remember. We met you and your wife at a cocktail party years ago." Gorgeous Anna, with Vince's hand on her ass. Who could forget?

"More like a lifetime ago. She walked out on me in 1984."

"I'm sorry."

"I used to be. And then I got angry." He rang the bicycle bell. "And then, eventually, I let go of her."

"Maybe I should get a bicycle bell."

He laughed. "Maybe, but they say a spouse's death is more traumatic than divorce."

"Actually, that's not why I was weeping."

"Oh?"

He had gray-green eyes, unblinkingly earnest. She felt gladdened by his gaze. "It's a long story," she said. "Long and complicated and self-centered."

"My kind of story."

A little tide of warmth climbed her chest. It was as if they had leapfrogged the small talk of a first conversation and were already deep into their fourth or fifth. "Would you. . . ?" She gestured toward the passenger seat, too embarrassed to finish the sentence.

"My pleasure."

He propped the bike against a tree and walked around the front of the car, unhurried, hands in the back pockets of his jeans. Slender. Salt-and-pepper hair curling over the collar of his shirt. "So," he said as he opened the door and folded onto the seat beside her, "start at the beginning."

READING THE AURAS

Contrary to all the advance billing, I've had damn little rest or peace since I arrived here. Granted, the setting exerts a certain charm. The ether shifts from one translucent shade of blue to another—aqua, azure, cerulean—in rhythm with the song of invisible birds. You can stroll along the billowy pathways unworried about cars, snakes and other mundane hazards.

But imagine greeting somebody who has no body. I spent a lifetime navigating (some would say blundering) among my friends and enemies, deciding whose smile to trust or breasts to ogle. Suddenly all those skills are obsolete. Now I have to converse telepathically with persons who are nothing but auras: radiantly colored, vaporous outlines of their former bodies. Believe me, it's disconcerting. I feel like an illiterate immigrant—a greenhorn, although I'm the color of smoke.

Not only that, the timelessness drives me nuts. No seasons, no hours, and of course no meals. I'm constantly checking a wristwatch that isn't there. Every now and then I sleep, only to wake after a while that could be ten hours or ten minutes. Nobody else seems perturbed, so who knows, maybe I'll get used to it. The sooner the better, because I hate drifting in this interminable meanwhile.

Worst of all, I'm still being nagged by the thousand regrets about what I should have done or, more often, shouldn't have—those if-onlys that form the psoriasis of the ego.

I know, I know, I should count my blessings, because it could have turned out far worse, but I've always been a glass-half-empty guy.

Nevertheless, I'm putting on a good face (or good aura) en route to the New Souls Orientation. Several dozen of us—every color and shape—have gathered by the entry gates, silent, still jetlagged by the transition. A rotund orange aura strides (if that's the right verb) toward us. "Hello there, I'm Dolly Johnston, but everyone calls me DJ, and in the next while I want to make you feel at home and happy here." Beaming, she shepherds us into a secluded area where we form a circle. "I bet many of you are feeling a little off-balance as you move around without your old packaging. That's perfectly natural. Don't worry: as your soul expands to fill up your aura, you'll feel more and more content. Whole-souled, that's what we call it. You may also be wondering why your aura is violet or pink or whatever. Well, to put it simply, each color signals a different mood and character. After a while you'll learn to read people by their color." She sends a few peachy blinks around the circle. "There's lots more I need to say, but first let's hear from you. For obvious reasons we can't use name tags." She trills a fluty laugh. "So I'll ask you to introduce yourselves, starting with this genial person."

"I am Arturo Salina," the beige aura across from me says. "Almost seventy-five years I lived in Milan, where I owned a jewelry shop. I had a happy family with my wife and four children and their children until the cancer came."

"Thank you, Arturo," DJ says. "By the way, I forgot to tell you folks, please don't talk about the past"

"I don't understand," someone says.

"The past is dead as a doornail," she says. "Trying to recollect it only hampers soul-growth. Stick to the present tense and, believe me, you'll become content. Now who's next for introductions?"

"My name is Deirdre," says a shapely pink aura, "and it's a pleasure to be here. I can't wait to know each and every one of you."

The group glows in unison.

Now it's blue aura's turn, but DJ points to me. "I notice you've gone a little burgundy, friend. Why are you feeling vexed?"

These damn auras—it's as if we're walking around naked, moodwise. "Vincent Delaney," I mutter. "I was a historian."

"Remember, Vince. Avoid the past."

"And that's exactly why I'm feeling vexed. I devoted my life to thinking about the past, and for good reason." *Stop,* I tell myself, but it's too late, I'm launched headlong into my annual opening lecture in the Age of Enlightenment course. "The present derives its meaning from the past. Birthdays, for example. Just like Americans celebrated their bicentennial birthday in 1976, every year each of us celebrate our private birthday." My aura is glowing like red-hot lava but I can't stop. "If you destroy history, if you erase memory, you'll wake up every morning with your brain washed clean and" (I try to mimic ripping up the syllabus and tossing the pieces over my students) "we'll become a nation of 300 million Alzheimer cases."

Silence. The newcomers look away, embarrassed or maybe angry, I can't tell one damn color from another.

"I apologize, folks. I'm a little jittery since the accident."

"You're forgiven, Vince," DJ says. "Everyone arrives with mental baggage. But after a soon while, I'm sure you'll find yourself better off without the past tense."

"I'm sure," I murmur. What I'm sure of, however, is that I've gotten off to a horrendously bad start on eternity. I picture Ellen across the dining room table nibbling an asparagus as I recount the diatribe I wish I hadn't delivered in faculty meeting. "Oh, sweetheart," she would say, "when will you learn?" Suddenly I feel that familiar breath-stopping ache lurch through my chest. The ache of love. But if my body has evaporated, how in hell am I feeling anything?

By the time I tune back into the New Souls Orientation, the introductions are over and DJ is saying, "so to help you through this first while, we've assigned each of you a guide. Now, I suggest you go to your niche and rest your soul."

· · ·

I'm trying to push the barking cat off the bed and grab the turquoise alarm clock, which is wagging madly, until I see the horizontal aura bouncing beside me and I remember where I am.

"Hi, I'm Annie," she says, shimmering a lovely blue-green.

"Who?"

"Annie, your guide dog. Didn't DJ tell you? I'm glad they assigned me to you. You can call me Sweet Girl. May I call you Vince?" She wiggles and bounces. "I see you're still a little sleepy but I just can't wait any longer to go out and about."

"Where are we going? And why a dog?"

"We're going to teach you to read auras, Vince. Someone who's turquoise, if I may be personal, is energetic, easily bored, and wanting to influence others. It sounds complicated but it's fun. And I'll help you. What do you think?"

Reading horoscopes, I think, *oh god, spare me,* but I do the equivalent of biting my tongue and say, "Cool."

"As for why a dog, that's easy." She rubs along my aura. "A dog is man's best friend."

I'm glowing orange where she rubbed.

"So, Vince, are you ready to go out and about?"

"Ready or not, here I come." My jaunty tone surprises me. After all, I've always been a cat person, a five-cat person, in fact, each one of them claiming to be the center of the universe, which made for a Rousseauvian state of nature in our household, but better that than the slavish neediness of a dog. "And one puppy in the family is enough," as Ellen remarked. But I have to admit, I find Annie endearing. Sweet Girl.

Out we go along the cloud-cushioned paths. Streams of people and animals—including, I swear to God, a pair of dolphins—meander in all directions amid a cheerful polyphony. I feel as if I've landed inside a well-mannered Hieronymus Bosch canvas. Annie chats with everyone, "hi, good to see you again, this is Vince Delaney, a new arrival," after which I try my hand, so to speak, at aura-reading. "I think he was peaceful, maybe a former gardener," I say about an emerald-green man.

"Good job, Vince, but did you notice a little gray around his edge? And watch out for your verb tense."

"Where's everybody going?"

"Nowhere in particular."

"And what else do they do besides walk?"

"Lots of things. Songfest is a favorite. And personally, I love Sublimity. But pay attention, because here comes Alexander."

Alexander's tall, sinuous, and pumpkin-orange. "My

pleasure, Vincent," he intones after introductions and banalities. "Let's make this the beginning of an endless conversation."

"Pompous," I say to Annie afterwards. "He used to be a politician or, who knows, a Princeton professor."

"Yes, a leader. Nice work. But his yellow halo means spirituality. Alexander's in charge of the Soul Center."

Good job? Nice work? Back in the Old Country she'd be feeding me little biscuits.

"I feel like one of my B-minus students."

She nuzzles me. "Don't worry about progress. The present goes on forever here."

"But all my life I've kept score. Little league baseball, Scrabble, academic promotions, you name it. Red-white-and-blue Americans believe in the *pursuit* of happiness. It's like chasing squirrels." Then I remember how she chatted with that family of squirrels. "Poor Annie. You got a tough assignment when you got me."

"Oh yeah?" She laughs. "Look at yourself, tough guy."

Indeed, sentimental pink blotches are breaking through the chocolate.

"Let's go home," she says.

In my niche she fits herself alongside me, a comma inside a parenthesis. The ether subsides into a steady azure. The birds sing their imperturbable chorale. Sweet Girl snores. I am at rest. At least temporarily.

In our next outing we encounter everyone from teenage

girls to a tribe of giddy penguins. I work my nonexistent butt off reading and misreading auras.

"Good job," Annie says. "

Frankly, I'd rather be reading a book in my office with a fresh cup of coffee and a doughnut. Or god forbid, a cigarette from the bottom desk drawer.

"Vince? What's wrong? You've lost your glow."

"I was remembering something."

"Don't worry. It takes a while to learn how to forget."

"What if I don't want to?"

She gazes up at me. "Come this way." We climb a hill to a niche overlooking the vast silvery cloudscape. Countless auras drift along the myriad pathways in mutating arrangements of iridescence. "Peaceful, isn't it?" she says.

I laugh, thinking of the night Ellen and I smoked marijuana the first time with the Schafers around their lava lamp and, two joints later, I remained sober as a priest. "I'm too conscientious to get stoned," I said, which sent them into a cascade of giggles.

"What's the joke," Annie asks.

"It's not fit for dog's ears."

The ether darkens, the birds trill, and I'm about to doze off when someone calls out, "Professor Delaney?" A green man is standing in front of me. "I'm Charles Weber, a former student of yours."

Just my luck. I could be meeting up with Rousseau or Karl Marx, but instead it's a former student. "Good to meet you, Charles." Well, at least I won't have to write a letter of recommendation.

"And I'm delighted to meet you, my favorite professor. French Revolution, right? Not that it matters any more." He laughs. "Who can imagine a revolution here?"

That's right, Charlie-boy, toss my life's work into the dustbin of history. "I'm still getting used to the place, as Sweet Girl will tell you." I look down, but she's across the path conversing with a pair of cats. "When did you arrive?"

"Quite a while ago, but who keeps count. No has-beens, that's my motto." He beams pistachio green.

Judging by the hunch of his aura, this former student died in his seventies. At least twenty years after my tricycle mishap. Which means I've been here longer than I realized. Years; decades. Holy shit. The sky is veering to the left, now the other way.

"Are you okay, Professor?"

"Annie!" I stagger toward her. "Take me home, Sweet Girl."

Spooned beside her in my niche, I instantly fall asleep, only to find myself in the old dream. I'm driving Ellen home from the hospital, the two of us happy as a couple of teenagers, until I look in the rearview mirror and see the empty back seat. "The baby!" I shout. "We've lost the baby." I drive like a maniac back to the hospital, run up endless flights of stairs, and stand at the nursery window. There's the crib with a tag, "Baby Delaney," and no one inside.

I snuggle tighter against Sweet Girl, wondering how I can outlast this merciless meanwhile.

. . .

After numerous outings, I can chat and read auras fluently. I'm no longer a greenhorn, but I'm the color of mustard: unsettled; in pain.

Annie's worried. "I don't understand what's wrong."

"I'm a slow learner. It took me years not to finish my book on Rousseau."

But she doesn't lighten up. "This may be something for Alexander at the Whole Soul Center. Are you up for that?"

So I'm being sent to the principal's office, or is it the chamber of the Grand Inquisitor? "What's he going to do to me?"

"Relax. He's really helpful."

All too soon we're at the entrance to the Center. "I'll wait for you here," she says.

I turn into a courtyard that shimmers in the golden glow of Alexander. "Make yourself comfortable over there, Vince." He's taller than I remembered, but his tone is even more pompous. "I gather you're having some acclimation problems."

"Apparently," I say, which seems nicely halfway between denial and agreement.

I prop myself on the ledge that serves as his version of a couch.

"Yes indeed. Judging by the indentation beneath you, I would say you're considerably underweight."

"What weight? I have no body."

"I'm referring to your soul. By now we would hope to have you filled up. Whole-souled."

"So those Jesuits were right after all."

"Pardon me?"

Time to give Alexander a taste of his own pompous medicine. "Near the end of the Middle Ages, a few theologians persuaded the king of France to grant permission for an experiment that had been forbidden by the Roman Catholic Church. They were allowed to weigh the soul of a criminal by comparing him before and after his hanging. Imagine what they found. The soul weighed an ounce and a half."

"How interesting." Alexander's aura has turned slightly tarnished. "Well, as I was saying, unfortunately you remain underweight. In my view, you're suffering from a backlog of nostalgia, compounded by regrets."

"And what can be done about that?"

"You have two choices. Ideally you and I work together on a regimen for expurgating those inhibitions. It's not as difficult as it sounds, and invariably successful. After an eventual while, you become whole-souled and settle in among us for eternity." He's back to pure golden glow.

"Or?"

He hesitates, makes a sound like throat-clearing, as if preparing for bad news. "Or you can choose repackaging."

"You mean return to life?"

"Yes, Vince. Start over, with a blank slate."

"Wow! A new life." I start blinking with excitement.

"But with the same old eventualities: hope and disappointment; pleasures gained and lost. Aging, frustration."

"And tricycle accidents."

"Exactly."

Silence.

"I don't know," I say finally. "I don't know. Let me think about it."

"As you wish."

Annie is jumping up and down as I come out of the Center. "You look better already, Vince. Isn't Alexander wonderful? What did he say?"

"He gave me a couple of different things I can do?"

"Great. Let's start now."

"Not yet, Sweet Girl. I need a little time to decide what I want."

We amble among the auras, nodding and murmuring, "hello, how are you, such a beautiful ether, see you at Sublimities," and the truth is, I know my decision. I'll resume and maybe this time I'll do it better, like teaching a course a second time. More kindness to others, fewer *faux pas*, and who knows, a couple of kids and a dog.

I'm a glutton for regrets. Starting with saying goodbye to Annie.